LITTLE BROTHER

They had been running for a long time now.

The two boys pounded through the forest, leaping over immense roots, twisting past dark bushes. They wore only torn and dirty grey rags around their waists and their skins were burnt to a deep coffee by too many months in the sun.

The smaller boy had felt as if he had been breathing fire for as far as he could remember, his legs trembling and shooting pain into his stomach with every unsteady step.

More than anything his body wanted to stop. It wanted to slide down to the ground and sink slowly into the gentle green moss. But he wanted to run faster, even faster. He knew he could not stop. Never.

"Historical novel, adventure, and character study, this book takes readers to another place and time, giving a sense of the culture and traditions of the Cambodian people and an even stronger sense of individual and family loss brought about by war."

— *Booklist*

Author's Note:
Cambodia was a quiet little country
lying between Vietnam, Laos and Thailand.
It became Kampuchea after the first of two bitter wars
and thousands of Cambodians, or Khmers,
have since been forced to leave.

Little Brother

ALLAN BAILLIE

PUFFIN BOOKS

My thanks to Mr Esmond Way of the
Sydney Indo–China Refugee Association and the people
of the International Red Cross at Aranyaprathet
for their help and guidance.

PUFFIN BOOKS
Published by the Penguin Group
Penguin Books USA Inc., 375 Hudson Street, New York, New York 10014, U.S.A.
Penguin Books Ltd, 27 Wrights Lane, London W8 5TZ, England
Penguin Books Australia Ltd, Ringwood, Victoria, Australia
Penguin Books Canada Ltd, 10 Alcorn Avenue, Toronto, Ontario, Canada M4V 3B2
Penguin Books (N.Z.) Ltd, 182–190 Wairau Road, Auckland 10, New Zealand

Penguin Books Ltd, Registered Offices: Harmondsworth, Middlesex, England

First published in Scotland by Blackie & Son, Ltd., 1985
First published in Australia by Penguin Books Australia Ltd., 1990
First published in the United States of America by Viking Penguin,
a division of Penguin Books USA Inc., 1992
Published in Puffin Books, 1994

1 3 5 7 9 10 8 6 4 2

Text copyright © Allan Baillie, 1985
Illustrations copyright © Elizabeth Honey, 1985
All rights reserved
Map by Andrew Mudryk

1. ESCAPE!

They had been running for a long time now.

The two boys pounded through the forest, leaping over immense roots, twisting past dark bushes. They wore only torn and dirty grey rags around the waist and their skins were burnt to deep coffee by too many months in the sun. They were lean, their muscles sliding under their skin like heavy wire. Both had eyebrows like black comets, a broad mouth, a short straight nose and darting brown eyes beneath tossing dark hair. The bigger boy was about eighteen and was constantly watching for a hiding place. The smaller boy was about eleven and wanted to curl up and scream.

The smaller boy had felt as if he had been breathing fire for as far as he could remember, his legs trembling and shooting pain into his stomach with every unsteady step. He ran blind to the great dark trees that roofed out the sky far over his head, locking his eyes on the feet of the bigger boy as they flitted through the tangled shadows. He heard only the bigger boy's breath thundering like a steam train on the flat, with his own strangled gasps drowned by the constant shouting and crashing behind him.

More than anything his body wanted to stop. It wanted to slide down to the ground and sink

slowly into the gentle green moss. But he wanted to run faster, even faster. He knew he could not stop. Ever.

Suddenly his foot slid sideways on a banyan root. He crossed his legs in a desperate effort to keep going, but he was moving too fast. He turned in the air and crashed heavily onto a dead branch. Immediately the sounds of men running seemed louder.

The bigger boy looked over his shoulder and wound his running to a skip and a stop in four strides. He turned back and propped his arms on his knees.

"Okay?" he panted.

The smaller boy scrabbled his feet under him, looking back at the noise with panic in his eyes. He spread his hands before him and levered himself to his feet, air sighing in his throat. He forced himself to start running, then staggered, and fell.

"My ankle . . ." he gasped.

The shouting swept through the trees towards them.

The bigger boy lifted his eyes from his mate, ignored his feeble efforts to get to his feet, and looked around him. After a few tense seconds he nodded at a nearby tree with a leaning trunk. He scooped up the struggling boy and half-dragged him to the base of the tree.

A man shouted angrily and threw himself at some brush twenty metres away.

The bigger boy skipped back from the tree and ran up the trunk, leaping at a low branch. He threw his legs over the branch and swung down like a

monkey to catch his mate's hands and pull him up. He pressed a finger on his own lips and waited, with the light, bony boy lying painfully across his back.

The thrashing swept round the tree in an angry tide. The smaller boy stopped breathing when a man paused directly below him. Through the leaves the boy could see no more than a foot in an old sandal and an arm in a black shirt, torn from the shoulder. The arm was carrying a rifle.

Suddenly the boy's right arm began to tremble, softly shaking the leaves on the branch. He grabbed his arm, bore down on it and bit it, tears flooding his cheeks.

After what seemed longer than a week someone in a distant tangle of vines called out and the man sighed, spat and moved on.

"All right, Vithy. Get off," the bigger boy whispered.

Vithy climbed off the boy's back very slowly and quietly. He could hear the soldiers moving away, but they were still too close.

"Now just be quiet."

For perhaps half an hour the two boys lay in the tree, motionless and silent. Then the bigger boy stretched and slid to the ground.

Vithy moved cautiously after him. "Are they gone?" he whispered. He rubbed the teeth mark remaining on his arm. "What d'you think, Mang?" Mang swung his arms about, freeing his cramped muscles. He looked at Vithy with an easy smile.

"I think, little brother, that we may have beaten them."

Vithy stared at Mang. Once, a very long time ago, he had resented Mang's smug 'big brother' attitude to him. But now Mang could call him—and did—a toad, a cockroach, as bone-headed as a water buffalo, anything he liked. Just so long as he was there.

Vithy tried the beginnings of a smile, the first since his furtive twitch when Mang had strolled into his guarded paddy months ago. "You think so? Really?"

"Why not?"

Vithy looked about him and listened to the forest. There was nothing now, not even the distant explosions that had distracted the soldiers and given them the chance to run. Nothing but the drowsy hum of fat insects and the call of a lonely bird. He began to relax, but clenched his fists again and could not stop watching the trees about them. They're coming back, he thought. Nobody ever beats the Khmer Rouge. But Mang hunkered beside him and squeezed his arm. "Hey, they're only a bunch of stupid mountain men. Let's have a look at that foot."

Vithy lifted his foot and leaned against the trunk. Maybe they can be beaten, this time. "You think they would have . . . shot us, Mang?"

Mang knelt before Vithy and felt around the foot. "Well they aren't going to shoot us now." Mang snapped his fingers as if he had forgotten something. "Hey, maybe they were taking us into the forest for a picnic. Eh? Fish and crab from the sea, pineapple and bananas and ice cream . . . Maybe we'd better go back."

Vithy laughed, and stopped. Laughter felt strange and he had forgotten how it sounded.

"I don't think it's broken."

"What?"

"The foot. Probably just sprained."

"Hey . . ." Vithy sat down with his foot stretched out before him. He looked astonished. "We're free."

"Sort of."

Vithy tried a bit of a giggle then a bit of a soft song to hear how they sounded. "We're not going to have to work in the Big Paddy any more . . . What do you mean, 'sort of'?"

Mang sighed. "Where are we, little brother?"

"We're . . . I don't know." Vithy looked alarmed for a moment, then recovered with a shrug. "Doesn't matter. You know where we are."

"We're still in trouble, little brother. Better, but still in trouble." Mang nodded in the direction of the morning's explosions. "At the paddy they were saying we're in some sort of war again. If we're careful we can get out of it, but we could get shot by anyone."

"Oh." Vithy was silent for a while, staring at the forest. "What do we do, Mang?" He was whispering again.

Mang shook his head. "I'm thinking."

"Do we go home?"

Mang looked at his brother. "You know we don't have a home any more . . ."

Vithy shrugged, then slowly nodded his head.

"Okay. We've got no time to think back. We go forward. Start again. Follow the lines out of the

10

war and everything." Mang stood up. "I think we'll go to the border."

"Which—?"

A shout echoed in the forest.

Mang looked sharply to his left and said very quickly: "They're back. Get down and don't move."

He ran off very fast, almost towards the shout.

Vithy pushed himself to his knees in a desperate attempt to follow him, but a man bellowed in triumph and Vithy dived behind a root. He watched Mang run across a small clearing, with shouts following him from almost a semi-circle. A shot echoed from near Vithy, then two more, but Mang was still running as he reached the trees on the other side of the clearing. Five distant figures ran across the clearing a few seconds later and other men pounded through the forest on Vithy's right. The shouting receded.

Vithy slowly raised his head and immediately felt exposed. He closed his eyes and pushed his face into the damp ground.

They'll come back, he thought. He ran his tongue over his lip. They'll come back when they see they are only chasing Mang.

He squirmed away from the tree to a cleft in the ground which was covered with dead leaves and roofed by ferns. He felt very cold and his arm was trembling again. He did not know whether he was afraid for Mang or just for himself.

It was probably just for himself.

But he knew what he had to do. Nothing. Mang had said, "Don't move!" and that was all he could

11

do. Mang would fool the soldiers; he always did, and then he would come back.

Vithy waited while the sounds of the searching soldiers died into silence and the hazy shadows lengthened. He tried to forget where he was and for a while he was in an old boat with Mang, shooting the rapids near home, scared stiff, and the boat half full of water, but Mang was whistling 'Old Man River', of all things . . .

Mang might not come back.

The dreamy smile died on Vithy's face and he was back in the forest. Why didn't he come back?

A single, distant shot.

Vithy stared at the echoing trees for a long, still moment, then cried out and jerked to his feet. He ran through the forest, his ankle sending bars of pain up his leg with every stride. He skipped, hopped, limped, shuffled, anything to carry him from the sound of the shot, his eyes awash and half blind. In the end he fell and rolled limply onto his back because he was too exhausted to keep moving.

He opened his eyes some time later to stare at clouds of leaves swaying darkly across an angry black sky. He realised where he was and turned away from the sudden memory of the shot, to see something like a grey lion about to roar from a bush a metre away.

He rolled away with a desperate gasp and had his good foot under him when he realised the lion threatening him was stone. Stone stained with algae and moss, cracked and bound together with vines. The lion was guarding the shell of an ancient temple slowly being destroyed by the coiling roots of a tall tree.

Thunder rolled above the shifting canopy of leaves and large drops of water splashed heavily around Vithy. He funnelled water from a broad leaf into his mouth, then moved into the complete darkness of the ruin, groping carefully as he went. He found a large flat stone, checking it with his fingertips as he sat. Outside the canopy swayed and creaked as water crashed onto the foliage. For a few seconds the canopy held the flood, then it rained lightly, then it poured.

Vithy stared at the curtain of water, and he imagined that if he could see through the rain he would be able to see what that terrible single shot had meant.

But he knew what it meant. It meant that he had no one, no friend, no family, nobody left. He was terribly alone.

Something moved above Vithy's head, sounding like worn leather. He crouched almost flat on the stone, staring up into the blackness.

Something like a mouse.

Vithy took in a shuddering breath, ready to scream. Two small eyes sparkled over his head. Then another pair, another and another until the dripping stone roof was watching him with a thousand eyes.

Oh, he thought, and relaxed. Bats.

As the night outside became a seething storm the roof above Vithy rippled, flapped and squeaked. Vithy lay on the rock and after a while he talked to the bats.

It stopped him thinking about Mang.

2. THE FOREST

Vithy woke to a gnawing hunger. That was normal. He would soon be shouted at by the soldiers, given a small bowl of rice and then marched out with all the other boys, men and women to work in the barren plain of the Big Paddy . . . But something was different.

There was a smell like damp mice and old stone. He opened his eyes, lay on his back and wondered where he was and why his ankle was throbbing. He called for Mang softly. Then he remembered and stopped. He wanted to close his eyes again and go back to a dreamless sleep, but the bats were stirring over his head. He limped slowly from the musky ruin to a silent forest still carrying a cloak of shining rain.

He drank from a hollow in a stone and walked from the ruin for a few metres, testing his foot gingerly with each step. He was frightened of the strange forest, the silence and above all the uncertainty of the day. He was so frightened he almost wanted to be back in the Big Paddy. There you could get killed for laughing or talking, but you knew the rules and there was a little food every day. Here, there was no food unless you could think how to find it, and Vithy had forgotten how to think.

Mang had told him, many months ago, that the only way to survive in the Big Paddy was to be careful and dumb. Work hard, never let them know that you can read and write and handle arithmetic. Always remember your kid sister, Sorei. And above all, never think. But now he had to.

Vithy leaned against a tree, which showered him. He was hungry, so hungry he could eat the bark from trees. If Mang was here he'd know how to get food. He always knew.

But Mang was dead.

Vithy slouched to the edge of a black pool and moved a long stick outlined by olive green algae in the pool. Maybe you could catch a fish. Maybe the pond wasn't big enough. Mang would know, but Mang was dead . . .

Was he?

Vithy blinked at the stick as if it had become a loaf of bread. He tasted the new thought carefully.

Was he?

Vithy picked up the stick and waved it at the ragged piece of sky over his head, his mouth open, his eyes alive.

No, he was not!

Some of the algae fell across his face and he sucked it from his lips.

They would never catch Mang. He was faster, smarter, stronger than they were, even now, even after a year in their paddy. It was only a single shot; that's all. They couldn't touch him with three shots across a clearing, how could they touch him in the middle of a forest? How could they keep up with him after half an hour? They couldn't; that's all.

15

Vithy tried to look into the pool, then probed it for depth with the stick.

And now he's gone back to the tree to find you!

Vithy dropped the stick.

Of course he has. Didn't he tell you not to move? He's there now, looking for you. Vithy turned as if to see the tree and Mang behind him. He took half a step from the pond and realised he could not find the tree again. Mang might stay by the tree for three weeks but he did not know in what direction nor how far away it was. He'd lost Mang as surely as if the soldiers had caught him.

Vithy turned back to the pond and picked up the stick to throw it as far as he could. Then he stopped, the green algae hanging from the black wood like jelly.

Mang had said something about a 'border', hadn't he?

Something like "follow the lines out of the war" to go to the border. What lines? Lines on a map? Telegraph lines? And what border?

Vithy's head was hurting, but that was all right. He was thinking again, and that felt good. He drew a big square in the mud round the pond with the stick. That was here, Kampuchea, full of Khmer Rouge soldiers trying to catch Mang. To the south there was the Gulf of Siam and the Pacific Ocean, and that surely didn't count as a border.

Vithy swept some algae from his hand and licked his fingers.

Now to the east there was the border with Vietnam and to the north was the border of Laos and they had wars about the same time as Kampuchea. To the west there is Thailand, which has not had a war with anyone . . .

Vithy leant thoughtfully, reached out for the algae, shook off some of the slime and opened his hand to look at the oily green mass. All he had to do was to find out where he was in that square, and which border Mang had meant, and go there to find him.

Vithy slapped the algae into his mouth, shuddered, and began to swallow.

Vithy found the forest a vast and lonely place in the next few days. In the beginning he tiptoed from tree to tree, listening for any sound that might be a warning and diving under a rock at a distant crash. But the only sign that people had been among the trees was an occasional partly overgrown path, and there was no sound beyond the chattering of monkeys, the gargling of a bird and the slow dripping of water.

There are no soldiers here, he told himself. And after a while he began to believe it. This forest was not all that different from the rolling country round his home at Sambor.

He woke on the third day in the forest to watch a small deer nibbling at a bush. He thought of trying to catch the deer, but a treeful of monkeys warned the deer and chattered at him until he walked away.

There are no soldiers here, he thought. There is no Big Paddy and maybe there hasn't been a war. Perhaps it's all been a bad dream, and Mang is behind the next tree.

He called for Mang a few times but there might be soldiers in the forest after all, so he stopped.

He ate a small piece of orange fungus on the fourth day and was wondering how to catch a monkey or a bird when he found a house. The house was built of timber and thatch, raised on thick stilts to three metres from the forest floor. It had shared a hollow with another house but the other house had been destroyed by fire a long time ago. Vithy stayed in the trees and watched the remaining house for an hour. When he was certain there was no one in the house he slid nervously out of hiding.

A loom and an unfinished piece of material collapsed like a tired dragon under the house. Parts of a badly rusted motor bike sprawled near the steps. And there was a vegetable garden at the back.

There wasn't much left. There had been a low mesh fence erected around the garden but animals had broken in and the forest had followed. Vithy found the stalks of a Chinese lettuce, three shoots of spring onion and a yam, which he ate as he found them, squatting on the earth and wiping them on his shirt. For the first time in a long while he wasn't feeling hungry.

He climbed the steps to the house. The front door sagged off its hinges; the house had been ransacked from the skeleton of its stove to its sleeping space and possession of the building was being fought out between spiders, birds and a tribe of monkeys. Vithy chased the outraged monkeys into the trees, cleared a wormed and cracked mat and slept under the soothing patter of rain on the roof.

Next morning he lay on his back and didn't want to go anywhere. The house was as comfortable and familiar to him as the palm of his hand and he didn't want to lose that feeling. He thought he might dig up the garden, see what he could find and plant some seeds and catch birds or something while they grew . . .

He got up and looked out at the quietly ticking forest as if he owned it. He picked a fragment of an old photo from the floor, a family around that motor bike when it was new.

That was it, of course, that was why the house had felt familiar. It reminded him of home, when Kampuchea was Cambodia and they were all Khmers and the Khmer Rouge were some bandits in the mountains and the war hadn't started. There was Dad's pet vegetable garden, his retreat when he wasn't working as a doctor; there was Mum's kitchen, but it had been white and shining with pots and pans; there was Sorei's corner of the kitchen, where she had talked with Mum for hours about cooking, Judge Rabbit, and how mean Vithy was to her; and there was even the motor bike down in Mang's 'Fix-it Shop' below, taken apart by Mang and Vithy time and again, and one day they'd get it to go . . .

Vithy carefully placed the torn photo on what there was of the stove, looked around at the battered old house, and left. The memories hurt too much.

3. THE ROAD

Vithy walked no more than a hundred metres along a muddy path before he reached a bitumen road. The road—any road—was menacing because it meant trucks full of soldiers at any minute and Vithy wanted to turn back to his safe forest. But he had to find Mang and he had to start by finding out where *he*, Vithy, was.

He stayed behind a tree and tried to work out where the road went. It was a year ago, but he could remember the Khmer Rouge making him, Mum, Sorei, Mang and eighty neighbours march south from Sambor for thirteen days. And the soldiers had then taken Mum, Sorei, him and forty-eight other people across the River Mekong, leaving Mang and the others on the other side . . .

For a moment Vithy's face loosened. Then he pressed his lips together and shook his head, as if to dislodge a thought.

"Okay," he told the tree.

Okay so they took Mum, Sorei and him to the Big Paddy. Forget about what happened there. Doesn't matter now. But he didn't know where the Big Paddy was for a start. Mang had joined him months ago, but yesterday soldiers marched them and some others into the forest for many hours—maybe to kill them because there wasn't enough rice—until someone started shelling the forest. They had run blindly from the soldiers in the confusion and he did not know how long they had run, nor in what direction. So he knew only that he was a long way south of Sambor, somewhere in the middle of Kampuchea. And west of the Mekong.

"What can you do with that?" he asked the tree.

He punched the tree, thought a bit and punched the tree again.

"Nothing," he said finally and started following the road to his right.

At first Vithy walked through the trees beside the road, but there seemed to be nothing on the road at all. It is slow, hard work to push through undergrowth with an open road beside you. And the road had been torn apart by craters and trenches, as if armies had fought with field guns for this strip of old bitumen. This must be why nobody was using the road: no truck could drive on it.

Vithy left the trees for the grass verge, and after less than an hour he was striding down the centre of the road with the confidence of a band on parade.

So he hopped and jumped down a chain of craters on a bend, and nearly stumbled into a truck.

The truck was painted khaki and heavily loaded. It was stationary. Four men, stripped to the waist, were working with picks and shovels to fill in a crater. A fully uniformed soldier was leaning against the truck, watching.

The officer looked up and saw Vithy. "Heya," he called.

21

Vithy ran very fast, very low into the forest. He tore into shrubs, weaved between trees, jumped a fallen log and hunched for the sound of shots.

But there were no shots at all.

Vithy's jagged race became a jog, then a panting rest. He trembled, swallowed and listened, but nobody was following him. He waited for an hour, and thought about what he had seen.

They wore uniforms.

Not black pyjamas, or pieces of uniforms like the Khmer Rouge he had known, but full brown uniforms from the caps to the boots. They were different. Go back and look.

Vithy closed his eyes and shook his head.

They're just stupid mountain men. That's what Mang said.

No!

In the end he crept slowly back to the road, his heart drumming in his ears. He had to know what they were.

The soldiers were levelling another crater as if nobody had ever seen him. They put their shirts on and the officer drove the truck off slowly. Too late Vithy smelt the bagged rice. He squinted after the truck and slowly worked things out. "Not the same soldiers," he said aloud, and walked onto the road to hunt for spilled rice.

A long while ago the Khmer Rouge had come down from the mountains of Cambodia, conquered the country and called it Kampuchea. Now, was it possible that some other army was conquering them? Did these soldiers fire the shells that gave Mang and him the chance to escape?

22

Vithy found five grains, put them in his mouth and sucked them as he walked on. By mid afternoon the forest had peeled away from the road and was replaced by huge rice paddies with no rice and no people. He heard engines revving on the road ahead and slid quietly through the paddies until the sound was far behind him. Then he returned to the road.

As the sun set he was beginning to pass houses, first singly, then groups and streets. A sign told him he was in the outskirts of Phnom Penh, the capital of Cambodia, but he could not believe it. He had known the river edge of Phnom Penh in festivals and a family holiday, and it had been a swirl of colour and noise, honking cars and revving motor bikes pushing against a river of people. But in this city everything was deserted.

Vithy walked on as the silence slid coldly up his spine. The buildings grew taller and crowded together as he moved into a darkening stone desert. The only sound he could hear was the nervous slap of his bare feet on the bitumen and the soft whispering of the wind in the streets. He thought of shouting at the city but he decided against it. What if some *thing* howled back?

Vithy stopped at a broad intersection and bit his lip. Now he knew exactly where he was and he wished he didn't. He had come here before the war with Dad, Mum and thousands of people for the music, lights and gaiety. Now there were only empty bandstands and stages in the long park to his right. To his left there were trains, long rows of slowly rusting metal, and beyond that there should have been a cathedral with an elephant grazing by its front door. Now, no elephant, no cathedral, nothing at all.

He walked slowly towards the centre of the city, feeling colder with each step. He passed many cars left by the side of the road, smashed, dented, sometimes burnt. A touch of wind whirled paper out of the gutter. Vithy was watching more paper money than he'd ever seen in his life littering the street. Awnings sagged from buildings with shattered windows and stained walls. Shops were bare and open.

Vithy reached the city's central market, a huge empty concrete dome, and looked for a place to sleep among the looted jewellers, tailors, radio shops. He entered a jeweller's shop through a kicked-in door and used a torn piece of curtain to sweep enough dust off the floor to sleep. He sprawled in the shadows and began to drift away from this city of ghosts . . .

"Eh! Come on. I can see you!"

4. KING OF THE CITY

Vithy jerked to his elbows as a shadow in the street rattled the screen over the window. He pushed himself desperately away from the shadow until he backed into a wall and was showered in glass. A piece of thin metal jabbed his finger and he grabbed it between his thumb and forefinger to defend himself. It was no bigger than a bottle top.

They had caught him. He knew they would.

"Oh, come on," the shadow said, waving something long and straight. Probably a gun.

Vithy thought wildly of throwing the piece of metal at the shadow and then running through the door. But it wouldn't work, and it would get them angry. He didn't want to get them angry.

"I don't know why I try. You're so dumb."

And for the first time Vithy heard the voice, not just the words. It was just a boy. No more than a kid. Vithy moved from the wall a little, but then he remembered all the small boys with high voices and guns he had met since the Khmer Rouge had marched down from the mountains. He pushed back to the wall again and bit his knuckles.

The boy sighed. "Look, you can stay there all the time. I don't care. Stay hungry." He turned from the window and walked away.

Vithy took his fist from his mouth and stared at

the empty window in blank astonishment. This sort of thing just never happened. A Khmer Rouge soldier who offered food and walked away from someone he had trapped? It was not possible.

"Wait . . ." Vithy stumbled to his feet, hurried to the door, tripped over a broken bar and fell into the street, holding his piece of metal as if it was a bayonet.

The boy turned and nodded at Vithy as if it was normal for him to be greeted that way. He walked back and plucked the metal from Vithy's hand. "Evenin'," he said. He did not look like a soldier.

"Hello," said Vithy cautiously, pushing himself to his feet. "I'm Vithy. You said something about food."

The boy moved into the moonlight to examine Vithy's piece of metal, and his bright gold and red shirt shimmered. He rubbed the metal against a sarong glinting with silver thread. "Where did you find this?"

Vithy was staring at the heavy gold chains round the boy's neck and wrists. "In there," he said lamely.

The boy raised the walking stick he had been carrying and pointed the handle at Vithy. "It's a little leaf from a brooch. Made of gold. Because you found it here, it's mine. All right?"

Vithy was looking at a savage elephant's head, carved in teak. But he managed to croak: "Why?"

"I'm the King of the City and you stink."

Vithy shrugged. He supposed he did, but there were so many other things to worry about.

"All right then? The gold?"

26

"Okay." It was a small price for a meal. But Vithy decided he was not going to be frightened any more by this kid. He relaxed.

The King of the City nodded and pulled at his lip. "Well, I suppose you want to eat first?"

Suddenly Vithy's mouth was in flood. The kid could call himself Emperor of the Universe for all he cared, just so long as he was the king of a bowl of rice. "You have something?"

The King laughed. "Come to my palace," he said.

Vithy followed the King past the concrete mountain of the central market, and began to expect a banquet. After all, a kid who wore enough gold to set up a treasury must have something. But it was a long walk, down silent alleys and streets to where French words began to appear on walls. They passed rotting green awnings where a fruit market had been and entered a building that had almost been destroyed by fire.

"This is your palace?" Vithy panted as he clambered over charred beams and broken bricks. Those dreams of fish and roast duck were steaming away.

The King winked. "It's secret." He groped for something in the floor, then swung up a small trapdoor. He led Vithy down a steep metal staircase into utter darkness that smelled of fish oil and kerosene. He stopped ahead of Vithy and fumbled while he muttered. A match flared and he persuaded an old lamp to light, throwing shadows into corners.

Vithy stared. And stared again.

"My treasure house," said the King.

The dusty cellar was jammed from floor to ceiling, from wall to wall with incredible riches. The King's swaying light washed over stacks of tins with labels curling brownly from the bright metal; tall jars of mysterious black fruit; crates of soft drinks and a careful stack of empty bottles; a long rack of shirts, belts and trousers, a TV set with a shirt drying on the indoor antenna; silver plates heaped in a corner; barrels, large cans of kerosene and vegetable oil, Indian rugs, a mahogany Buddha, a rattan ball, even a brand new bicycle.

"Where'd you get all this?" Vithy waved his arms about.

"From my City," said the King, dusting an Indian rug with his hand. He motioned Vithy to sit. "What would you like to eat?"

Vithy was getting annoyed with the boy and his queer game, but then he looked at the stacked tins of pears, baked beans, lychees, beef stew. "Ah, anything," he said, touching his lips with the tip of his tongue.

"Caviar, eh? Maybe venison soup. No, at the start." He opened a tin of potato salad and poured it onto a silver plate. "I'd turn the TV on and give us a bit of entertainment, but we don't have any electricity."

Vithy took a spoon from the King and placed his little piece of metal on the rug. He began to shovel the salad into his mouth.

"And we don't have a TV station either, or a tap that works. We wash in the river. I don't suppose you can fix things."

Vithy could not talk, had to keep eating until the

29

salad was no more than a smear on the silver. He shrugged.

"Like an outboard motor."

"Sometimes." Vithy forced the word through a full mouth.

The King smiled at Vithy and opened another tin—pears—and joined him. This time Vithy could talk between mouthfuls.

"Where's everyone?" he said.

The King shrugged. "All gone. After the war the Khmer Rouge marched in and kicked them all out."

"Oh." Like Sambor. Did it happen everywhere? The Khmer Rouge bandits come down from the mountains and fight the government. After the war they are the government and they say everyone who lives in a city or a town has to go to the country and plant rice. *Everyone?*

"But I stayed. Nobody shoves me around. If I don't want to go I don't go. Once they see me, they try to catch me but I am a cyclo man. I know—"

"What . . .?" Vithy finished the last pear and felt beautifully heavy inside. He wasn't really listening.

The King clicked his tongue in annoyance. "Cyclo man, cyclo man. Rickshaw with a bicycle. What, you come from the mountains or something?"

"I know it. My brother and me, we fix them a lot at home."

"Yes, well I'm a cyclo man and I know this city like a mouse knows his hole. They never catch me and I go around the city and fill my palace. I stay and they're gone so I'm King of the City."

30

"No soldiers here?"

"Not the Khmer Rouge. I say 'Go!' and they go. Off to fight another war."

"Who against?"

"Where you been? It's the Viets this time. The Khmer Rouge attacked some Vietnamese villages, or something, and it's war again."

Vithy leaned back and nodded. Vietnamese. They were the soldiers with the truck. End of mystery. And that's one border Mang wouldn't go to.

The King took off his splendid shirt, changed his silver-threaded sarong for a black and grey rag, took off his sandals and stood up. "Now for a wash. Why have you come here?"

Vithy told the King about Mang and the escape through the forest as the boys climbed out of the cellar and walked down a street to the river.

"You really are looking for him?" The King poised on a landing.

"Yes." Vithy took off his rag, smelt it and threw it away. The King was right.

"You'll never find him." The King plunged into the dark water.

Vithy jumped in after him, feeling the cold water lift weeks of sweat, dirt and weariness from him in a second. "Why?" he yelled.

"Where would he go? He could go anywhere. If he came here, even I might not be able to find him. But he might be anywhere. Or dead."

"He's not dead!" Vithy shouted.

"All right, all right, take it easy. Have some soap."

Vithy caught the slimy white object and began to

lather. He turned in the water and looked at the black city sitting on the black river beneath a single spray of stars. It wasn't the city he had known. The sullen stone shapes were strangers to him, hostile and secret.

He swam to the King's side in a last clutch of hope. "Mang said something about a border . . ."

The King laughed and kick-dived to the depths of the river. He stayed under for almost a minute and spouted like a whale when he broke surface. "What border?"

"He didn't have time to say."

"Well, there's the border with Laos . . ." He pointed across the river. "That's more than three hundred kilometres away and you'd have to cross the Tonle Sap and the Mekong for a start. Or the border with Thailand. That's maybe four hundred kilometres away and you'll have to go through the war to get there. And then where are you going to look? It's more than six hundred kilometres long from the sea to the mountains. And there's Vietnam . . ."

"There's lines at this border," Vithy said in desperation.

"And tigers too, maybe?"

"Well he said they were there."

"'Course they are there. That's what a border is. Cross the line and you cross the border and you're in another country."

"Oh," said Vithy. There was something he should have remembered, but it remained just out of reach. "All right."

The King nodded sympathetically. "Look, you don't need a brother. You don't need anyone at all."

5. RIVER OF GOLD

Vithy slept high in the King's palace that night, in a room with a hole for a window and very little roof. He lay on his back looking at the stars and tried to think about Mang and how he would never see him again, but he was just too tired. He woke to the sun rising over the river and the smell of fish frying. The King had found a tin of kippers in tomato sauce and was cooking them with rice over a portable gas burner. When he had finished eating Vithy would follow the King anywhere.

They did not go far. The King found a simple shirt, shorts and a pair of new sandals for Vithy, then he picked up his rattan ball, walked outside to a clear space in the street and kicked it to Vithy.

"Can you play?"

Vithy instinctively stopped the ball with his knee. "Not any more." He dropped it to the inside of his right foot and skied it towards the King. The effort hurt: he hadn't used those muscles that way for a long time.

"Ah, come on, you're better than a brick wall." The King swung his hip at the ball.

"I'm terribly stiff." Vithy danced back to meet the ball and missed. That annoyed him. He missed twice more in the next three minutes, bounced the ball erratically away from the King five times and then caught the rhythm.

The two boys danced around each other, whistling, clapping, singing little songs with the ball always spinning in the air. Vithy would sky it with his head, then slap it with the sole of his right foot, left knee, left shoulder, right toe, hip, nose, side of leg, heel and back to the clapping King. And for a while he was grinning again.

They moved from the ruined shops to large stone houses in avenues with tall trees, then to the quiet park surrounding the hill, the Phnom. They collapsed by the many-headed stone serpents guarding the stairway to the top of the Phnom and laughed.

"I think I am dead," Vithy panted, when he had recovered enough breath to speak at all.

"That was fun," said the King. "I will allow you to stay in my City."

"Why, thank you very much."

The King arched an eyebrow and sat up. "Up the top, then."

Vithy looked at the distant temple or *wat* at the top of the Phnom and groaned. "Why?"

"To see if there are any trespassers." The King got up and carried his ball like a royal orb for the first few steps.

They climbed past tall and broken park lights, past the stained *stupas*, immense stone ice-cream cones thrust into the earth, past the canopies of trees and finally reached the small and battered *wat* sitting on top of the Phnom.

"Wasn't that worth it?" said the King.

The Phnom was only a small hill, but the entire city was as flat as a dinner table. Vithy could see down a broad road to the monument on the other side of town. Pagodas glittered gold and green in the sun, and the central market was now a flashing white. Buildings had been destroyed and broken glass looked like ponds in the roads, but the city no longer seemed frightening.

"I used to wait outside that big building, over there, for most of my business," said the King. "Hotel Royale, always full of reporters and photographers from all over the world."

"In those days you weren't a king?" Vithy was smiling.

"Better than that. They'd come to me and say, 'Ang, take us to the best restaurant, or a crime boss, or the best money black market or where the Khmer Rouge blew up the Tonle Sap bridge.' And they knew that I knew where it all was . . ."

"Soldiers!" shouted Vithy and threw himself on the ground.

Something big and fast was boiling along the road from the monument.

The King peered at the approaching army truck and raised his hand in a lazy wave. He squatted by Vithy. "You are really hung up about the Khmer Rouge, aren't you?"

Vithy turned his head on the gravel and looked up at the King. "They are very bad."

"You were at one of their rice farms, weren't you? What was it like?"

Vithy shook his head. He did not want to talk or think about the Big Paddy.

35

"How long were you there? With just your brother?"

Vithy pressed his lips together. He wanted to pull the King down beside him and get him to shut up. "A year. With my mother, and my sister and Mang."

"And now you are just looking for Mang. Only Mang."

The two boys looked at each other in silence. Then the King turned away and stood up.

"Get down!" Vithy hissed. "They'll see you!"

"Ah, it's all right. They're Viets. I allow them to come."

Vithy very cautiously picked himself up and watched the truck reach the sweeping circular road round the Phnom. It could have been the same truck Vithy had run from, what—yesterday?

The truck squealed half way round the circle and sped away from the Phnom as suddenly as it had come. Vithy began to relax, then saw the truck's destination.

"There's a ship," he said in astonishment.

The ship was sitting in the river, very close to the shore and less than a kilometre from Vithy, but through the buildings he saw little more than a funnel with a vapour of steam escaping, some white superstructure and a white flag with a red cross on it.

The King waved it away. "It's unloading rice. I let them come and go. Let's catch some fish."

Vithy followed the King as he skipped down the steps and walked to the river. "But where's it from?"

36

"What? Oh, that one? I think it's from France."

The King wasn't interested in ships or soldiers in the City, so after a while Vithy gave up asking questions. They walked along the river bank until the King stopped by a crumpled tarpaulin. He pulled it away to reveal an old but newly painted boat, ready loaded with net, and a long-shafted outboard motor.

"Can you fix that?" said the King.

Vithy knelt by the small motor and lifted the cover. To fix a motor Mang would examine it like Dad with a patient and ask Vithy for tools. But now there was no Mang, and Vithy didn't think he knew what to look for.

"It'll take a little time," Vithy said. "Got any tools?"

The King drew a blue tool box from under the net. "Tell you what, we'll paddle out. I catch fish, you fix the motor and we zoom back."

"If we're lucky," said Vithy gloomily.

They pushed off from shore and paddled away from the city, to where the river became a motionless lake of deep gold. The King cast his net at the dying sun and caught a handful of fish while Vithy fiddled with a spring.

Vithy looked up from the motor in exasperation and was surprised to remember that he had been here before. On a riverboat with Mang, Dad, Mum and Sorei on this particular patch of water. On his left there was the city and the Tonle Sap river, flowing very slowly from the Great Lake, the Tonle Sap, and on his right the mighty Mekong and home. If you went down the Mekong for long

37

enough you would reach Vietnam and Ho Chi
Minh City, once Saigon. If you went up the
Mekong for long enough you would reach Laos,
then China and even the Himalayas, but before
Laos you would reach Sambor. Home.

"Where you from?" said the King.

"Sambor." And now Vithy was remembering
Sambor before the Khmer Rouge, before the war,
before the generals who threw out the Prince and
started everything. When it was a very sleepy little
town with a market, pagodas, rice, fish, boat races
and the family. Once upon a time.

"I been there," the King said, "where the road
stops. I love the river. Was working on one of the
riverboats, all the way from Phnom Penh to Kratie.
One trip I went past Sambor to see the rapids.
D'you ever see the Prek Patang Rapids?"

"I went down them, with Mang."

"Not in the wet."

Vithy smiled and shook his head. "No. Not in
the wet."

In the wet the Mekong turned from a lazy village
dog into a roaring monster. It seethed over the
rapids, plucked stilted houses from its banks and
often flooded the streets of Sambor. Every year it
poured into the Tonle Sap river and forced that
river to change direction and flow back into the
Great Lake. You didn't do much on the Mekong in
the wet.

But when the rain stopped the Mekong calmed
and dropped, leaving millions of fish in the Great
Lake and rich new soil on the paddies. And the
Tonle Sap river changed direction again, to flow

39

into the Mekong. And in the old days Cambodia celebrated with a great Water Festival at its capital, Phnom Penh.

Vithy sat up in the boat and remembered how it was just before the Prince was overthrown and the war began. How the family crowded into the riverboat, with most of Sambor, to cheer Mang and the rest of the dragon boat team on to victory. All the way down the Mekong with the riverboat going pocketapocketa and Dad, the dignified Doctor Muong, playing the Pan pipes of a *khene* while he danced with the others. Until they reached the city.

Vithy turned to look at the city, and from this far out Phnom Penh had not changed. It still looked like something out of a story book, with gold and green roofs glittering in the sun. The Royal Palace gleamed like wet marble and—who knows—the Prince might be in, the monks might be walking past in their orange robes and the people, thousands of them, might be gathering before the palace for the boat races.

"It was good, wasn't it?" the King said.

Vithy looked at the King in surprise and then realised that they had both been thinking of the same thing. He smiled at the King. "You know, Mang was in a crew that almost beat the Prince's boat . . ."

The King hurled a piece of black wood into the river. "That brother again. Do you ever do anything without him?"

"You don't have a brother?"

"I don't have anyone."

"I'm sorry."

The King ran the net through his fingers. "I never had anyone. Just me."

Vithy looked at the King for a long time and tried to think of something to say.

In the end the King shrugged and said: "I suppose it must be different with a family, eh?"

Vithy stared at the bright shell of the empty city. "Mang is all I've got now."

The King nodded once and hauled in the empty throwing net. Vithy pulled the cord on the outboard motor a few times before it coughed, shuddered and pushed the boat across the golden water. The King looked at the vibrating motor in surprise but did not speak during the return journey.

They reached the city as the sun set behind the pink walls of the palace, dragged the boat up from the river and covered it with the tarpaulin. The King lay the motor on his shoulder and began to walk to his 'palace'.

"I suppose you better find him," the King said.

6. THE TRUCK

Vithy shuffled behind the King towards the soldier, instinctively shrinking as he approached and with his legs quivering, ready to run. His hands were sweaty.

But this soldier smiled. He looked up from a list he was making and waved a pencil at the king. "Eh, Ang? Hungry enough to work?"

The King shrugged. "What you got?"

"The same. Who's your friend?"

"Vithy. Wants to load your trucks."

"Always room for one more."

Vithy realised he was being spoken to and looked up nervously. He had been catching the heavy scent of pork and noodles—almost as good as last night's fish—and he was fascinated by the boots on the soldier's feet. They were even polished. "Yes," he said lamely.

"Good. I'm Sergeant Trang. You work with us, you eat with us. The morning meal is round the corner. You better be quick, before it's all gone." The sergeant waved the King and Vithy away.

Round the corner of the river-shed there was a huge steaming cauldron, a few soldiers eating in a huddled group and—to Vithy's surprise—about thirty-five Cambodians, in rags but waving chopsticks at him in greeting. Cambodians, Kam-

42

pucheans, not Khmer Rouge but just Khmers, his people. Vithy quickly scanned the faces, from the old man with the single tooth to the tough little girl, but Mang was not among them.

"My City is getting crowded again," muttered the King, and moved towards the cauldron.

Vithy ate two bowls of pork, fish, noodles and greens answering and asking questions between mouthfuls and staring at the white ship with the red cross a few metres away. It was the greatest ship he had ever seen, almost fifty metres long.

No, nobody had seen Mang.

"He might be at the border," said the tough little girl, and shovelled her mouth full of rice.

Vithy stopped eating and looked quickly at the King. His reason for working on the Viet trucks was supposed to be a closely guarded secret, but a grimy girl of no more than eight was almost telling the world.

"Which border?" said the King with a shrug.

"The Thai border, of course, Ang. There's refugee camps there." The girl sniffed.

"Ah, you're so smart, Monkey. That border is more than a thousand kilometres long. Where would you start looking?"

The girl shrugged and left the King in triumphant relief.

But a long thin man squatting beside Vithy said: "Aranyaprathet. That's the closest Thai town to here, maybe five hundred kilometres away, and it has camps all round it."

The girl beamed over her rice. "Maybe you could catch a truck," she said.

Vithy hung his head and heard the King groan.

After the meal the Khmers began to earn their meal and Vithy started looking for the right truck. The ship was being unloaded at the same time as the loading of army trucks. The King and Vithy ignored the ship and spent the day heaving bags of rice, noodles, milk powder and corn onto trucks and learning where they were going. They could not get rid of the feeling that all the Khmers and all the Vietnamese soldiers were watching their every move.

The King had altered his earlier ideas on the chances of Vithy ever finding Mang, but not by much. He had decided that Mang would head west for the Thai border, even narrowing that border down to Aranyaprathet. And there were trucks constantly leaving Phnom Penh for places west and nearer to the border—if you were fast and sneaky enough to catch one. But there was fighting everywhere between the Vietnamese army and the Khmer Rouge and the fighting had concentrated on the Thai border, with shelling, tanks and troop battles.

Vithy was able to forget about the fighting while he was looking for trucks, but a small part of him was hoping he wouldn't ever find the right truck. That small part of him was very happy when he found that one truck was going to Kompong Speu, almost a suburb of Phnom Penh, and the second and third trucks were both going south to Takeo, not west. After that the boys were too exhausted to carry one more handful of rice. They collapsed on the bank of the Tonle Sap, gazed at the wrecked concrete river bridge and waited for enough strength to eat their Viet army dinner and trail off home.

A final truck creaked in from the road, backed up to a pile of sacks and stopped.

The King shook his head. "No. Definitely not."

The sergeant clapped his hands. "One more truck, then you can go home!" he yelled at the Khmers lounging round a rice pot. Someone muttered.

"Where's it for?" asked the King.

"Does where it's going make the sacks lighter? Siem Reap. Come on, come on."

Vithy sat up and stared at the truck, excited but with something prickling up his back. Dad had often talked of Siem Reap. It was near the ancient ruined city of Angkor, where he and Mum had worked and danced before he became a doctor, and is about three hundred kilometres out west. Less than two hundred kilometres from Aranyaprathet.

"All right," sighed the King, "after dinner."

Most of the Khmers had left to sleep in the city. Vithy and the King quickly spread palm leaves before them and ladled hot rice and some curried fish on them. They rolled the leaves to form four large green sausages, tied them with twine then slung them from Vithy's shoulders under his shirt. They ate from the pot hurriedly for ten minutes then joined the two men loading the truck.

The King whispered something to the men. They nodded then resumed work. Now the men would heave the sacks up from the wharf and the boys would stack them, sack after sack of rice and corn, on the tray of the truck. Under the sergeant's

45

eye the work was innocent but slow, but when he drifted off the King rolled a sack away to reveal a dark cavity.

"Now," he said and Vithy jumped for the hole.

Vithy squirmed into a sitting position among the sacks and looked up. "Why don't you come with me? Out of the war and everything."

The King laughed. "And leave my City? Oh, no."

"Well, thanks . . ."

The King rolled the sack over the hole, plunging Vithy into darkness.

Vithy rolled the words he had just said round his mouth, and frowned. "Out of the war and everything," he had said. Mang had said those words in the forest. "Follow the lines out of the war." Not "cross the line" as if it was a border drawn in the mud, but "follow the lines", as if—

The sack was suddenly rolled aside and the King thrust a plastic bottle into Vithy's hands. "You should have thought of this. It's water." He frowned at Vithy and for the first time since Vithy had known him he looked uncertain for a moment. Then he shrugged, pulled something from his pocket and pressed it into Vithy's palm. "This is for fixing the motor. So long, stupid."

He slammed the sack back and began heaving other sacks over the small hole. Vithy ran his fingers over the serrated edge of the gold leaf. He did not think of borders or lines again for a long time.

Vithy heard a man take his place in the final loading of the truck. The man talked and joked with the

46

King as they worked but neither spoke to or about Vithy. He felt as lonely as he had been in the forest after Mang had gone, but this time he was still within an arm's reach of a friend. It felt far worse when the loading was finished and the truck was left alone in the night.

He sat in silence for a long time, fighting to breathe the heavy corn-laden air and thinking of the Khmer Rouge lying in the dark forests and waiting for him. The taste of the air became bad and it was getting hot. The sweat gathered on his back, neck, forehead, and poured from his nose. He was only prevented from pushing the sacks away from the top of his head and giving up by the thought that the sergeant would see him and punish the King for helping him. He sipped some of the water in the plastic bottle and tried to imagine himself floating in the Tonle Sap.

Suddenly two men clambered onto the truck and Vithy held his breath. He was certain they were about to search for him. When he heard the metal click of a gun he opened his mouth to scream. The sacks over his head sagged under a man's weight . . . and a man yawned.

The truck slid out of the city, through a busy area with many men shouting at each other and heavy vehicles moving slowly, then accelerated to forty kilometres per hour on the smooth bitumen. Cool air filtered between the sacks, coating Vithy's face with corn and rice husks but drying out his body and feeding him with air that was almost fresh. He began to get excited. At this rate they would get to Siem Reap in the morning, he might even beat Mang to the border . . .

The truck slowed, and stopped. The engine died and the soldiers leapt down from the sacks, leaving Vithy alone and anxious. He knew this could not be Siem Reap. It was far, far too soon. Perhaps the sergeant was lying when he said the truck was going to Siem Reap. Or perhaps it had just gone to the war and the Khmer Rouge were all round and the soldiers would unload the truck in a minute, and catch him.

After half an hour the soldiers climbed back on board and were joined by three others, all laughing. The engine was switched on, the brake released and the truck rolled slowly down to a road of creaking wood. A bridge? Then the truck engine was switched off and a clanking engine started with a gasp and a hiss. The truck and the wooden road moved slowly and very gently. They were crossing the Tonle Sap on a ferry, because the bridge had been destroyed. Vithy relaxed again.

The truck moved off the ferry and drove quickly down the road for ten minutes before it stopped again. Someone on the road talked to the driver and a sack was thrown down to the road. The truck moved off again, but it soon wandered all over the road as if five people were fighting for possession of the wheel, or the driver had been shot. Vithy was alarmed until the truck lurched and swayed like a log in a flood.

Of course, he thought. It's the road. It could take a week to reach Siem Reap.

But after a while Vithy became used to the erratic movements of the truck and went to sleep. He dreamed that Dad, Mang and he were chasing a

48

duck, shuffling together with their hands out-stretched as if in a comic dance. They were all laughing . . .

". . . Khmer Rouge?"

The tautly whispered phrase plucked Vithy from warm Sambor and threw him back into the truck, awake and afraid. The truck had stopped, but the motor was being kept at a fast idle. Vithy could hear the sound of guns being cocked. Someone called from a distance ahead and the driver called back. The truck edged forward. A soldier was moving his body cautiously across the sacks that covered Vithy's hole.

The man on the road shouted in Khmer for a few minutes, something about five families and a dry paddy. The driver shouted back and the man over Vithy's head sighed and eased to the rear of the truck. Two bags were dumped on the road. The truck moved on, but Vithy knew that it was a matter of time before one of the soldiers took the sacks hiding him to give to people on the road.

Vithy tried to work out how far he had gone, whether it was still night or morning. He sucked at his water bottle and found that by pushing back on the sacks he could catch a little light. It was morning and the truck was probably above the Tonle Sap and passing the Tonle Sap lake. They were half way there.

The driver drove the truck faster now, hurling it across craters he would have skirted cautiously during the night. Vithy saw the sack over his head slip and hurriedly propped it while he slowly eased it back to its right place. On one suicidal downslope he was banging on the walls of his hole rather than the bottom, and with every impact of his body on the sacks a little dust cloud escaped from the hessian. The air in his hole was getting foggy with floating particles and he was constantly fighting back the urge to sneeze.

But the truck did stop for a long time in a makeshift army camp. Vithy moved the roof sack far enough to look around and decided that this was not Siem Reap. He stayed put while he finished the last of his water and breathed better air. He closed his hole as the soldiers wandered back to the truck twenty minutes later.

After a while Vithy's dim light began to fade. It must be the end of the day and Siem Reap must be getting close. He must get ready for a dash to freedom past the soldiers. He flexed his legs and a ball of pain shot up his right leg. He bit his lip to stop himself from shouting and rubbed his legs until they tingled, but he didn't know whether he could move them at all at Siem Reap.

The test came sooner than he had expected. Once again the road became smooth, the engine accelerated and the truck skidded badly round a corner. Sacks were thrown from one side of the truck to the other, one soldier was nearly catapulted to the road . . .

And Vithy was tipped from his hole.

"Eih!" A young soldier squealed in surprise and pointed. Another soldier reached for the body that had been dumped at his feet.

Vithy didn't wait. He rolled over two sacks and leapt from the truck.

50

7. THE BICYCLE

Vithy rolled along the road like a flung coin. He tumbled until he could spread his arms and legs in the dust, jerking himself to his feet and trying to run. He listened for the shouting and the shots as he reeled sideways, ran, fell and ran again. But when he turned he saw the soldiers just sitting in the truck, staring at him as they disappeared round a distant bend.

Vithy stopped in the middle of the road and coughed until rice husks stopped tickling his throat. He was picking grit from his skin near a street of shattered shops and a sluggish canal when he saw a cyclo parked in the long shadows near the canal. He walked towards it with growing excitement.

The cyclo couldn't be much different from the one the King once rode round Phnom Penh. It was an old bicycle with its front fork bolted to a wheeled seat with a folded canopy, so that instead of having two wheels this cycle had three. But it was badly browned with rust, the wheels were missing several spokes and there were torn flaps trailing from the canopy. This cyclo could be abandoned, and maybe Vithy could ride it all the way to the border . . .

Vithy stopped in the middle of the road when he

saw a leg dangling over the canopy. He looked hard at the shadowy seat and made out the long form of a sleeping youth. Then the youth opened one eye.

"Ah . . . hello," Vithy said.

"Um." The youth closed his eye again.

Vithy hefted the banana leaf sausages around his neck. "Is this Siem Reap?"

The youth opened both eyes. "Used to be. You a tourist? Want to see Angkor?" He laughed. "Where you from?"

"Phnom Penh."

"Long way. You want the border."

Vithy was surprised and it showed on his face.

"So many people trying to reach Thailand. Now there aren't many left."

"Are there any lines or something at this border?"

"Lines. Oh sure. Lines of people, our people, trying to get out of the country. Like I said. Why?"

Vithy smiled for an instant. This time it fitted. Follow the lines of people. Vithy's smile died as he realised that this could be anywhere on the six hundred kilometre border with Thailand. "How do you get there?"

The youth jerked his thumb past the street of shops. "Just follow the sun."

Vithy pressed his hands together and bowed his head. "Thank you. Ah, are there any other bikes around?"

The youth looked at Vithy shrewdly. "No. They're all gone."

"Oh." Vithy half-turned away in disappointment, then remembered the King's last gift to him. "Can I buy this one from you?"

The youth threw his head back and laughed, rocking his cyclo and slapping his palm on the mudguard.

Vithy waited patiently for the storm of laughter to subside. "I was not making a joke."

"But you were!" the youth spluttered. He gasped for air. "What were you going to use to buy my beautiful cyclo? The rice around your neck, your clothes, your sandals, maybe a million paper riels?"

"I have a little gold."

The grin disappeared from the youth's face. "Let me see."

Vithy looked at the youth. The youth was bigger and stronger and older than he was. He could take the gold leaf from him and ride away. There was nothing he could do about it. But how can you buy a bicycle without showing the price you could pay? You just have to take a chance.

Vithy pulled the leaf from his shirt pocket and passed it to the youth. The youth held the leaf between his first finger and his thumb, raised it to the setting sun and flicked it to spin, a flashing spark of gold in his hand.

"Do you have any more?" the youth asked.

"No." Vithy watched the spinning leaf and the gold light flickering across the youth's face.

The youth threw the leaf into the air, and caught it. "It's not enough."

Vithy nodded sadly. He had lost his gamble and he knew it was a useless gesture when he held out his hand. "Can I have my leaf back then?"

The youth opened his hand, then closed it and waved a finger at Vithy. "Tell you what I'll do. I've got a yard full of old bikes. For the gold I'll let you build your own. Hop in."

The youth climbed from the passenger seat to the saddle without touching the ground. He put the gold leaf into his own pocket, leaving Vithy with little alternative but to climb on board. The youth rode off along the side of the canal.

They passed many clusters of bamboo waterwheels straddling the canal. Many of them were jammed with weed or broken, but sometimes a wheel four times Vithy's height was still turning, scooping water from the canal and pouring it into a wooden pipe. The pipe carried the water to a dark jungle of weeds, turning what had once been a paddy into a swamp.

The youth stopped at a shambles of a house, a wreck that had been sagging and shifting before the war and now had no windows, no door, a hole in the roof and the paint was peeling off the plaster board. But the youth took Vithy into the back yard with an air of pride. In the back yard there was a graveyard of motor bike parts, motor scooter parts, skeletons of cyclos and rental bicycles. Tins half-full of grease, bottles of oil, wheels upon wheels upon wheels with tyres and tubes hanging from rusty rods.

"Okay then?" said the youth.

"It's a lot." Vithy stared at the bits and pieces of thirty bicycles and again wished Mang were here. Mang could stand here and work out exactly which part went with which to build a bike and how long it would take to do the job. He could build a bike out of almost anything, but he wasn't here . . .

But sometimes Vithy would fix a bike all by himself. Maybe he had learned enough.

"Thanks. It's okay," Vithy said.

"Big business when the tourists were here. They'd take a bicycle to see Angkor and crash and the bicycle would have to be repaired. Now you can use anything you find here and you can live here while you're working."

"Yes . . ." Vithy had a sudden doubt. "This is your house?"

The youth shook his head. "Nobody owns anything any more." He flicked the leaf into the air and snatched it. "Goodbye." He walked back to his cyclo.

A sudden idea flicked into Vithy's mind. "Wait a minute . . ." He ran after the youth.

The youth climbed onto the cyclo and turned to face Vithy warily. "What? You can't have it back."

"No, no, that's not it. I was just thinking. With all the people you see going to the border, have you seen my brother?"

The youth laughed and shook his head. "Maybe. Who knows? There's hundreds of people going to the border. How would I know?"

"Well, he looks like me, only bigger . . ."

The youth smiled and framed Vithy's face with his fingers. "Let me see now . . ." And the smile disappeared. "Um, might be."

"Did you see him?" Vithy pushed forward in excitement. "Did you see him?"

"Might've been him. On the back of a truck

56

going towards the border maybe four days ago. Whistling. Might be." The youth shrugged and mounted his cyclo.

"What was he whistling?"

"Oh, I don't know. Anyway, it wasn't Khmer. It was stuff you hear from the tourists. When they were here. But you couldn't tell. He was a terrible whistler." The youth shook his head and rode away.

Vithy raised his arm and started to shout for the youth to come back, but he stopped. He knew all he wanted to know. He turned from the road and wandered over the yard and the house without seeing much and with a quick skipping step.

He could see Mang paddling in the rapids of the Mekong grinning and whistling so out of tune it sounded like a balloon going down. Whistling 'Ol' Man River' like the tourists.

Vithy tried to whistle the way Mang had done as he took off his three sausages of rice and put them in a cupboard but it couldn't be done. He was even grinning as he walked across the road to the canal and stepped straight off the bank into the shining black water.

"I know where I am," he sang, and ducked to the cool clean water under the scum. "I know where everyone is."

He swam slowly under a waterfall created by a big but broken waterwheel, took off his clothes and scrubbed them clean.

He was now no more than a few days behind Mang, who had not been shot in the forest but was waiting for him up ahead. All Vithy had to do now was to catch him.

57

While he was under the gently tumbling water Vithy felt he could run the hundred and fifty kilometres to the border that very night.

He woke in the house at dawn with gravel gashes throbbing on his shoulders and knees, a dull ache at the base of his spine, a weary pain in all his muscles and a hunger so acute he could bite wood. He brushed cockroaches off the sausages and managed to limit himself to eating a third of one. He did not know where or when he would find another meal. He found that one tap would give water, so he drank a lot before he began to build his bike.

He started off well. He found a frame intact, with the front fork still attached and enough paint to keep the rust at bay. He found a paint tin with a few tools among the weeds and the snails. He found a complete set of pedals on a broken frame, but it took him two hours, a great deal of effort and a badly bruised finger to remove the pedal crank from the frame, and he lost two ball bearings when he unscrewed the cones. He decided then to collect everything he was going to need before he went on with the building of the bike.

He quickly found two wheels of slightly different diameters and with only a few spokes missing. In two badly mangled frames he found two axles which would fit those wheels and wondered what the tourists had been doing on the bikes. He even found mudguards and screws. He found a chain so rigid with dust that he could carry it like a pole. He found a tyre and a tube that fitted the rear wheel perfectly, and several pumps, but the only other

tube that could hold any air was too big for the
front wheel. He selected a damaged tyre to go with
the tube and reluctantly discarded the first wheel in
favour of a wheel that swayed with a buckle and
needed eight new spokes. He could not find a
handlebar anywhere.

Vithy ate the second third of the rice sausage in
the house and relaxed, listening to the creaking of
the big waterwheel as it patiently and uselessly
scooped up water, lifted it high and poured it back
into the canal. If he closed his eyes he could almost
imagine the splashing was the murmur of the
Mekong outside his house.

He suddenly remembered that there was one
thing he had been able to do better than Mang: be a
special friend to Sorei. She would find him under
the fig tree, trailing her broken doll behind her, and
ask him to fix it. Him, not Mang, because he was
young enough to listen and old enough to help,
while Mang was too big, too grown-up and he
called her 'kid'. So they sat in the shade of the fig
tree and fixed the doll, discussed the mystery of her
latest Judge Rabbit tale, laughed at elephant jokes
and plotted darkly the fall of the snooty girl from
Phnom Penh, who always pretended she was an
important lady . . .

Vithy sat up and wiped his arm across his eyes.
He hurried from the house and walked about his
gleaming junk yard, kicking metal shapes as he
moved. He did not sleep for more than an hour.

He was awakened very early next morning by a
man and a woman shouting at each other as they
walked down the street. Something about coming

home to nothing. Vithy lay motionless on the floor until they had passed his house, then sat up, wide-eyed.

As the youth had said, nobody owns anything anymore—until the original owner comes back. If the owner of this house returned while he was still building the bike, what could he do? It wasn't his, he didn't have anything to buy the parts he was using. He would lose the bike and all the work he was doing would be wasted.

And what was to stop the youth from coming back to claim the bike as his own?

Vithy hurried to the pile of scrap that would be his bike and started work silently in the dark. He fished the rusty chain from a tin of dirty oil and found that he could move it almost easily now. He hung the chain over the tin to drip and began to assemble the rear wheel. By the time the sun had pushed its rim over the rooftop the rear wheel was ticking smoothly in its fork. Vithy sprawled in the shade of a tall clump of bamboo and finished his first rice sausage before he looked for enough spokes to straighten the front wheel.

He wondered where Mang was now, and whether he'd seen Angkor on his way through Siem Reap. After all, it had been Dad's dream city, Mum's dancing stage and it was so close. But maybe not. Why stop and get the memories back? He'd have shot straight for the border, and he'd be waiting there now. He'd better be.

Vithy returned to his bike and began to gather spokes. He broke two, inserted four in the wheel and tuned the rim almost like a piano. He snapped

60

another spoke, kicked the wheel and worked for forty-five minutes to replace it. The wheel still wobbled but it did not touch the fork and that would have to do.

There was a small puncture in the tube for the front wheel, but he found a hard, topless tube of rubber glue. There was a small pocket of glue that had not yet set. He cut a patch of rubber from one hanging tube, repaired the puncture and waited for the glue to set. He looked again for a set of handlebars, but all he could find was half a handlebar and another folded in upon itself. He tried to straighten the folded handlebar, realised that it would break and hurled it away.

He walked across to the canal, toppled into the water and drank for a long time. He thought how good it would be just to float away, past the broken wheels and into the inland sea of the Tonle Sap. But he had no time.

He returned to his inner tube and pumped it up enough to listen for escaping air. The tube was silent so he deflated it, fingered it into place between the rim and the tyre and used two flat spanners as levers to fit the tyre. He pumped up the tyre, fitted the front wheel and turned the bike the right way up. For a few minutes he sat on the saddle and felt the bike move under him. If only he had handlebars . . .

And then he stared at the clump of bamboo over his head. A forest of handlebars. He went to the bamboo with the blunt and broken blade he had used to cut out the rubber patch, selected a pole taller than the house and began to cut.

The sun was setting now, and Vithy ached all over his body. He just wanted to eat some of the remaining rice and sleep. But he was so close now and that boy could come to claim the bike in the morning. Vithy worked on in the fading light for two more hours. Finally he stood back with his dead arms hanging before him like the arms of a big monkey, and he could not straighten his back.

But the bike was ready. A chipped yellow frame, half a silver front mudguard, no rear mudguard, a black front wheel, a rear wheel that was red with rust, no brakes at all and a sawn-off piece of bamboo rammed into the eye of the steering column and held there by a piece of grey rag and three pieces of wood hammered into place. Not a beautiful bicycle at all, but it was his.

Vithy went into the house for the last time, and slung the rice sausages across his shoulders. He came outside, picked his shirt from a rusty pole and sat on the bike while he buttoned it. He listened to the slow creaking and splashing of the big wheel then pushed unsteadily on the pedals.

And the ugly collection of bolts, rubber and old metal changed. Within ten metres the bike had steadied on the road and a sudden breeze was whispering behind Vithy's ears. The tyres hissed softly on the bitumen, the spokes whirred through the heavy air and the chain slid silkily beside Vithy's leg.

Vithy sat proudly on his creation and felt that it could fly.

8. DREAM CITY

Vithy would have ridden smoothly out of Siem Reap and slept by the road to the border but for the sign. He skirted a few soldiers round a low fire, turned for the road east, and saw the old discoloured tourist sign by the canal pointing towards Angkor. He stopped.

He did not want to see the old ruins. Dad had talked about them off and on for as long as he could remember and Vithy could picture the huge temples of Angkor Wat and the Bayon, the beautiful stone *Apsara* girls and the walls of elephants without seeing them. Angkor would be just like the house in the forest, with sad memories at every step. No, he didn't want to see Angkor.

But Dad and Mum had always promised to take the whole family to the place where they had met. They had hung gold and black rubbings from the walls in every room of the house and they talked as if they had built the ancient city themselves. Vithy was so close, they would not have liked him to miss the city and he was now leaving Cambodia, perhaps for ever. He would have to go. Vithy rode into the dark for about ten minutes, reached an open space with a moat around a dark building and went to sleep under a tree.

He was snapped awake by water exploding on

his face. He sat up in confusion and fingered water from his eyes as heavy rain swept over him. After two seconds of the slanting, stinging rain he was as wet as if he had fallen in the canal. He shrugged, opened his mouth, sat in the mud and tried to remember where he was. The rain eased a little, a grey curtain lifting from the trees, and there was some great walled city swimming in the jungle, as if it would disappear in the next wave of rain. Just like that.

Vithy stood up in the mud and peered across a moat that was broad enough to be a small lake. A causeway of worn stone slabs crossed the moat and passed a long mottled wall to reach a grim city of massive stairways, gateways as tall as trees, galleries of so many columns they looked like a picket fence, and towers like great lotus buds scraping the low cloud. But it wasn't a city, just one building of a city that had been a ruin for more than five hundred years.

Vithy mounted his bike and rode slowly across the causeway to Angkor Wat. Until this moment he had felt that Angkor was a fairy tale, a myth like the snake-god that had changed into a prince. Oh, Angkor Wat was on the flag of Cambodia in the good times, you could see photos of the ancient city every day and there was no such thing as a book on Cambodia without Angkor, but it was all so unreal.

And Dad hadn't helped. A hundred years ago, Dad said, a French explorer pushed through a dense jungle and found a great city that everyone had forgotten about. A city built a thousand years ago

with towers of gold, a vast treasury filled with tribute from Thailand, Vietnam, Laos and Burma. A city of great walls, canals, reservoirs, and buildings with towers made of the mighty faces of kings. And the kings rode to battle on elephants with a thousand soldiers around them . . . Who could believe such a city existed?

Vithy stopped before a flat stone area in front of the building, and realised with a low thrill that this must be where Mum had danced. He could even see the battling elephants on the wall she had talked about. She would glide out of the shadows, glittering in her green and gold costume, and tell ancient tales with her hands and her eyebrows. The other girls would follow her and they all would be the legendary dancing girls of Angkor, the *Apsara*. The spotlights would play over the high towers, the elephants on the wall, the long row of columns, and the tourists would applaud. Among the tourists would be Dad. Almost every time Mum danced, he said.

Vithy left his bike long enough to see two stone *Apsara* prancing at each other on a wall, but he felt that anything could happen to the bike while he was away from it. He returned to the bike and rode back across the causeway and deeper into the city of Angkor. He passed through a mighty elephant gate guarded by stone giants pulling on a *naga*, a seven-headed serpent like the monsters on the hill at Phnom Penh.

After the French explorer found the ruined city of Angkor, archaeologists cut back the jungle and carefully began to rebuild the city. Khmers carried

66

immense carved stones clear of a ruin, archaeologists worked out where they had been before they fell and the Khmers lifted them back. And Dad was there, making chalk marks on the stones, helping out until the Phnom Penh university opened and taught him how to be a doctor.

Vithy stopped before a tumbled mountain of rocks, blinked, and was staring at tower upon tower of four-faced stone heads. The heads were bigger than Vithy's entire body and some of them made him look like a gnat. This was the Bayon, and Dad and Mum would creep into its halls at night to make rubbings from the carvings on the walls for the house they were going to have.

And just a few metres beyond the Bayon was Dad's workplace. He had spoken of a parade of stone elephants being built from the rubble of centuries and this was it. Mum would come in the late morning and sit on the Elephant Terrace to watch Dad and ten other Khmers lifting a block to complete a trumpeting elephant on the wall. Then Dad and Mum would sit on the roots of a banyan tree and eat a rice sausage and drink burnt sugar water. It must have been a very good place with laughter and people everywhere recreating a city as grand as Rome . . .

Vithy leaned forward on his bike and smiled as he imagined the bustle around Dad and Mum just a few years ago, and the thunder of a thousand years before as the elephants of the Khmers cleared the jungle for Angkor. But Vithy started to listen and the smile slowly withered on his face.

Angkor now was as quiet and desolate as Phnom

Penh had been when he walked into it; as haunted and as dead.

He turned his bike from the Elephant Terrace and rode out of the city.

9. THIEF!

The road from Siem Reap was deserted at first. Vithy could see people working in paddies a long way from the road and he could not tell if there were soldiers with the people. There was nobody close to the road. He got used to it, but he did not like it at all. After an hour he saw something on the road, so far ahead it was no more than a speck floating above the road. The speck grew to a family, or two families, as he approached and everyone was tired. A thin man stopped Vithy by putting his hands on the handlebars.

"You come from Siem Reap?" the man said.

Vithy nodded. He was nervous.

"Are they still fighting?"

Vithy blinked.

"The soldiers," a woman carrying a baby was almost shouting in his ear, "are they still there?"

The man turned on the woman. "You shut up."

"Oh, yes, they are." Vithy saw the woman's face fall. "But they're not fighting any more."

"Ah. Then the Khmer Rouge . . .?"

"They're gone."

The man let go Vithy's bike. "These soldiers. Did they bother you?"

"No."

The man gnawed his lip as he turned to the others. "It's still soldiers. It might be trouble."

"We have to find out, ei?" said the woman and marched past Vithy's bike. The others followed and the man shrugged and went after them.

Vithy rode into rolling hills and past a few other people walking towards Siem Reap. They all had that tired, hunted look about them and they all asked the same questions. Around midday he rode into a small deserted village, where a house was on fire.

He dismounted in the middle of the main street and walked slowly towards the fire. The house had been burning for a long while now; it had staggered forward and collapsed in a black pile of broken wreckage, filling the street with dark stinging smoke and spitting at the drizzle. Vithy called out softly a few times, then he smelt meat cooking. He followed his nose, almost running beside his bike, until he reached a slab of bullock meat being barbecued over a low fire, with nobody in sight.

"Hello?" Vithy stood three metres from the most delicious meal he had ever seen or smelt and called for its owner. Nobody answered and after three attempts he dropped his bike in the mud and tore at the meat, burning his fingers. The meat was very tough but it tasted so rich and heavy that Vithy just stood before the barbecue with his eyes closed, swaying.

Then he started thinking.

Who would kill a bullock, a village's tractor and truck, just for a few meals? Why did they leave part of it cooking? Were they being chased? Who was

70

chasing them? Would they come back? When? Who had burned down the house? Why? Who . . .?

Vithy tore off another double handful of meat, shoved it into the banana leaf sausage with his last few grains of rice and rode from the village very fast. After that village he did not want to be seen by anyone. He spent the afternoon hiding in a quarry and rode only at night. He heaved his bike up the endless hills slowly, carefully and always listening for the sound of people. Any people at all.

But toward the end of Vithy's second night of riding he strained up his last tortuous mountain. Then he stopped pedalling and sped down a chain of slopes and humps, skidding round tight bends with black drops at his front wheel, the wind plucking at his shirt and streaming it behind him. Once he shouted in fright as he almost hit a log on the road, but the gnawing fear of the deserted village was behind him now. He was going too fast even for the Khmer Rouge . . .

So he stayed on the road as the sky began to lighten and stopped in a silent town with a sign-post. He had reached Sisophon. To his left was Battambang and another way back to Phnom Penh. But to his right was the Thai town of Aranyaprathet. The border was less than forty-one kilometres away.

Vithy looked at the rim of the rising sun. Ride on a little bit, he told himself, sleep the day and tomorrow you reach the border.

He rode through Sisophon humming, and out to the flat derelict paddy country with a rusty railway running by the road. He could see some blue hills far ahead and wondered if they were really Thailand.

He looked again at the disused railway track and with a sudden prickling behind his ears realised what he was looking at. The railway had once carried great trains from Phnom Penh to Bangkok until the wars had stopped them and pitted the tracks with rust. But they were still railway tracks, railway *lines*. Follow these lines, the only railway to cross the Cambodian border, and Mang would be waiting.

Vithy shouted in triumph and sped his bike down the road to the blue hills of Thailand. He would keep on riding today, reach the border tonight, find Mang tonight. Do everything today. It's possible. Anything's possible.

Suddenly a dark shape rose from the grass beside the road and rushed to Vithy's bike. Vithy gasped in surprise, turned the bike away and jumped on a pedal, but the bike was seized and shaken in anger.

Vithy was staring at a gaunt woman with hard, glittering eyes and a knife in her hand.

"Get off!" The woman thrust the knife a thumbnail's width from his throat. "Get off. Get off!"

Vithy jerked his hands from the bamboo handlebars as he recoiled from the knife and the woman's eyes.

The woman hit him hard in the face with her forearm and he spun from the bike with a shout of pain. She glanced down briefly at his sprawled body before turning away.

Then she mounted Vithy's bike and rode rapidly towards the border.

10. THE CART

Vithy sat up in a puddle and watched the bike he had created from a scrapyard disappear down the road. He fingered his nose, where the woman had hit him, but he wasn't angry, just hurt and surprised. Once upon a time he might have been shocked by some adult stealing a bike from a kid—especially him—but he had seen a lot since then. Now he accepted the theft as just one of those things, something that was his fault because he could have stayed off the road in daytime.

He got up, shrugged and walked on. Of course, it was going to be harder and longer to get to the border. There was no meat or rice left and it would take him two days of walking to reach it. Oh, he'd get there all right, but it would have been so much easier if he had been Mang. If he had been Mang the woman would never have thought of taking his bike, would she? Everything is easier for big kids. Small kids have to be smarter . . .

Vithy was hoping that the woman would fall off his bike and break a leg when something snorted at him. He turned to see a slow bullock pulling a cart carrying a load of firewood and an old man with a tailless monkey on his shoulder.

The old man touched the brim of his straw hat

with his prod and smiled. "Ah, we might've got past you, you're so much asleep . . . Going to the border?"

Vithy nodded.

"There's nowhere else to go. C'mon up." He stretched his hand down to Vithy.

The bullock looked hard at Vithy, as if it could smell yesterday's meat in his breath. Vithy hesitated. "Ah, I am too heavy."

"Don't worry. Naga can pull an elephant off its feet. You're a flea." He caught Vithy's wrist and flicked him casually up onto the cart. "What's your name?"

Vithy told him. The bullock looked back at Vithy and snorted, but it continued its rolling gait. The monkey scratched its chin as it studied Vithy gravely.

"Are *you* going to the border?" Vithy asked. He tried a smile for the monkey but was met with an irritated click of its teeth.

The old man scratched his knee. "I go close, but not there. You know there's trouble ahead."

Vithy's arm suddenly trembled. He leant on it. "What?"

The old man raised a finger. "Listen."

Vithy stopped breathing and he could hear a faint rumble like a distant storm. He had heard it before, just before Mang and he had broken from the Khmer Rouge soldiers in the forest. Before he had been running from the sound, but this time he was going right into it. "Fighting?" he said.

"It comes and it goes. Two armies out there, between us and Thailand. They fight when they find each other. This road goes straight into Thailand but you cannot follow it."

Vithy stared far ahead, at the empty road and the peaceful blue hills. Just waiting for him. "There's soldiers?"

"Many of them. Big guns, lorries, tanks. Everything. It's a war."

"Then how do I reach the border?"

"I do not know."

Vithy felt a great wave of weariness. He was too hungry, his nose throbbed, his legs ached so much he was sure they were going to drop off. He did not want to go on.

The old man scratched the monkey's head. "Maybe you better forget about the border. Why you want to go to Thailand anyway? Better stay with us."

"Us?" A family, a village? Mang was a long way away.

The old man waved his hand over the cart and the bullock and the monkey. "We have a house. Not much good, but it is a house. We even have two ducks."

Not a village, not even a family, just the old man and the monkey, and the bullock. And two ducks. But it was a place, wasn't it? Vithy remembered feeding the family ducks at Sambor. Not two, but a yard of frantic birds, flapping, clacking their beaks angrily at each other as he moved among them with a bowl of grain. Dad was chasing them from his vegetable patch all the time, shouting, waving a stick. Then Vithy was a little god and the whole world was under his control. Sorei grew up a bit and took over the ducks and of course he was too old to feed ducks now . . . but, still . . .

Vithy smiled and shook hands with the monkey. They were beginning to make friends. "What do you call the monkey?"

The old man glared down at Vithy. "She is not a monkey. She is an ape. A gibbon ape. See, no tail."

"Sorry. I forgot."

"She is Apsara."

"Apsara?" Vithy remembered the stone dancing girls in Angkor. And Mum. He looked at the ape and slowly smiled as he pictured the ape in the sparkling green and gold costume and towering head-dress Mum had worn. He grinned, and suddenly giggled.

The old man looked down his nose. "You do not think she is Apsara?" He snapped his fingers. "Dance, Apsara. Dance."

The ape bared a tooth at Vithy and somersaulted casually to the broad back of Naga. Totally ignored by the bullock, Apsara spun, swayed to an ancient rhythm, wobbled her head and became the evil and all-powerful Monkey God. She flipped several times in the air and clapped her hands until she had Vithy clapping his and laughing so hard tears were running down his cheeks.

But suddenly Apsara stopped her dance and leapt from Naga's back to the old man's lap. The old man turned to see two trucks roaring towards the cart. The first truck slowed beside the cart and thirty soldiers were looking hard at Vithy.

"Where you go?" The officer in the cabin spoke with an effort and a heavy accent.

The old man bowed his head. "Only to my house."

"You are going to the Khmer Rouge."

The old man stiffened his neck. "No. never."

"What are you carrying?"

The old man passed his arm over his load of firewood. "As you see." He jerked lightly on the reins.

Naga stopped in a slow step and the truck rolled forward. The officer hesitated, then motioned the trucks on their way.

"Leeches," said the old man. And smiled.

The old man flicked his prod and Naga leaned forward very slowly until the cart began to move. Naga accelerated with the casual power of a great train leaving a station, but only to the speed of a man walking fast. After one gentle hill Naga moved from the road to a rutted track without any sign from the old man.

"Apsara, coco," said the old man.

Apsara immediately turned and burrowed beneath the firewood. She disappeared, then reappeared with a yellow coconut in her hands. She gave it to the old man and pulled an old metal spike from behind the seat. She held it point upwards against the seat as the old man punched a hole in the coconut. Then the three of them shared the rich clear milk.

"We have to hide things now," the old man said, "from thieves and leeches. Apsara and me, we know where there's coconut trees, and sweet potatoes, even bananas. But we have to keep them hidden, eh?"

"Mang and me, we used to hide things in our special tree," Vithy said, feeling the coconut milk coursing down to his waiting belly. "Nobody knew about it. We once found an old gold watch and hid it there, but it disappeared. Mang said it was *phis*, spirits of the forest . . ."

"Who is Mang?"

"My brother. I'm going to find him over the border."

"Oh," said the old man.

They split open the coconut and ate the white flesh and Vithy talked about Phnom Penh, the great ship in the Mekong, the house in the forest and his escape from the paddy with Mang. But the old man didn't say much at all. The sun slowly closed Vithy's eyes and the cart was rocking gently like a fishing boat. He finally slumped back with his mouth open and a piece of half-eaten coconut on his lap.

Vithy awoke with the old man's hand on his shoulder. It was still light but there were a few stars in the sky.

"I think you leave now."

Vithy straightened his back and his neck felt as if someone had been beating it with a club.

"Listen."

Vithy sat up and looked at a low range of jungled hills, a dark green shadow in the twilight. Very peaceful, except for someone setting off crackers a long way away.

"A battle?" He spoke in a faint whisper.

The old man shook his head. "Just a squabble.

79

But it is far ahead, nothing to worry about. I hear some fighting in the hills behind us, but there is no fighting out there tonight." He pointed at the forest straight out from the cart.

Vithy breathed in. "You think I should go?"

The old man smiled. "You have a brother."

"Goodbye, then." Vithy stared at the sullen hills and thought of an easy life with the gentle old man and his ape. It was all so safe . . .

"Goodbye." The old man was looking straight ahead.

Vithy closed his eyes and jumped from the cart.

"Vithy?" the old man called after him.

Vithy turned.

"Be very careful."

Vithy nodded and walked into the forest.

11. THE BORDER

For ten minutes Vithy crashed through the undergrowth as if he was being chased, then he turned.
He wasn't sure what he was looking for; maybe he
wanted to see the old man for the last time, or
maybe he wanted to be called back, but the forest
had closed behind him. He was once again completely alone in a forest full of enemies.

He stopped and listened. The forest was
breathing, ticking, rustling, chattering quietly to
itself, but there was nothing he could see beyond
the dark columns of the trees. He was being
watched.

Vithy pressed against a tree and a lone night
bird wailed from a hill. He shook his head in
disgust. Of course he was being watched. The
insects were watching him; the monkeys were
watching him; the birds were watching him.

And he told himself, they had better. Because *he*
was the most dangerous animal in the forest.
Nothing frightened him at all. Really. They had
better remember that. He took a deep breath and
strode from the tree he had been hiding behind.

After half an hour of pushing through dry
undergrowth, trying to ignore the terrible din he
was making, Vithy found a track and the forest
opened up. He began humming softly . . .

The shots were so close they seemed to explode inside Vithy's head.

He threw himself to the ground and clapped his hands over his ears. He could still hear the savage chop-chopping of several guns no more than fifty metres away, the gasping of the bullets and the splintering of wounded timber. He could hear running feet on the path and he rolled quickly into the undergrowth. They had caught him. They had let him go in the forest just to wait for him here. They had been playing games with him.

Vithy heard the panting runners before he saw them. Then two men jerked towards him, clawing at the air as if they were trying to swim. He slithered into a trembling runner's crouch in the bushes.

No. Don't move. Just don't move.

They passed him and a man stumbled close on their heels, looking backwards to a woman with a small girl held to her shoulder. The little girl was screaming, but she stopped when she saw Vithy and stared at him with enormous eyes until she was bounced out of sight. Then a stream of old men and women with a few children. Last was a teenage girl trying to run with a one-legged man. She saw Vithy's face in the bush, frowned, opened her mouth and ran on. A gun coughed from a tree and the girl swayed but kept moving. Vithy bit his forearm but did not move. Maybe, just maybe, they don't know you're here. Lie still.

There was no more shooting. The pounding on the path receded but there was a rustling in the forest all around him. A man laughed briefly, a gun clicked and the rustling faded away.

Vithy remained motionless until well after the insects had begun to murmur again. He slowly relaxed his legs, rested his head on his arms and allowed his arms to tremble. He listened to the beat of his own heart and ran his fingers over a pebble until it began to shine dully. But finally he knew there were no soldiers near him any more.

He stood up, carefully brushing the sticks from his shirt, and listened. When nothing changed he moved along the path, from tree to tree, holding himself in a hunch between the trees. But as he crept through the forest his confidence seeped back. He could almost see the border beyond the next trees. A slow shuffle became a walk, a sweeping stride, then a tiptoe run. He could not be stopped now.

He tripped over something lying across the path, stumbled, but kept running. He had glimpsed only a black shadow as he had passed over it, touched it with his foot for an instant, but that 'something' nagged at his memory as he ran.

It was a body.

How could he tell? Just a few more minutes and he would be at the border, past the Khmer Rouge for ever and with Mang.

It was a woman.

Don't be stupid. It was a log covered with vines.

It was a woman with long black hair fallen across her face.

If it was a woman, she's dead and there's nothing you can do.

She's alive.

How can you tell? Look, there's soldiers every-

83

where. They can probably hear you running. You're almost there.

She *might* be alive.

Look, what do you want? People aren't expected to do things now. Things aren't normal any more. It's a war and people just look after themselves. Like the woman who stole your bike . . .

Like the old man with the coconut? Like the King with your piece of gold?

Vithy slowed down and stopped with a sigh.

He walked back and found the teenage girl with her mouth open and her eyes closed. There was no sign of the one-legged man she had been helping. Vithy bent over her, with a peculiar mix of feelings, sorrow and the hope that she would be dead and he could run on to the border.

Then she coughed.

"I've got to go . . ." Vithy muttered. But he knelt by the girl.

The girl looked as if she was peacefully asleep with her long eyelashes resting on her cheeks and her ribs moving very slowly under her black dress. But her shoulder was covered in blood and she was still bleeding. Left alone, she would die in an hour.

But what could he do?

Once a Meo, a mountain hunter, ran up to Dad and pleaded for help when he, Mang and Vithy had been looking for a Buddhist ruin in the mountains near Sambor. The Meo said a friend's old rifle had exploded when he pulled the trigger. What could Dad do, Mang wanted to know. This time there was no medicine bag, no nearby clinic.

"There's a nearby jungle," Dad said. "That

84

might do." So the Meo's friend was carried to safety on a stretcher made of vines and branches, drugged with herbs, and his wounds treated with other drugs and black mud . . .

Vithy looked round hurriedly and ran to a nearby bank of moss. He carefully lifted a ragged square of moss from the bank and carried it back to the girl with both hands. He gently tore her dress from her shoulder and stopped the suddenly increasing flow of blood by pressing the moss over the wound. He moved his fingers over her shoulder and found that the bullet had missed her shoulder-blade but had broken her collar-bone.

He stood up, took his shirt off and tore it into broad strips and placed them beside the girl. He collected some palm leaves, placed them over the darkening moss and tied a bandage around her body to keep the moss and palm leaves in place. He tied loose loops round her shoulders and scrubbed her face with moss until she woke.

The girl opened her eyes, closed them again in pain and flicked them wide and staring. "Please," she groaned.

Vithy recognized the fear. "No soldier. I am Muong Vithy. Can you sit up?"

The girl relaxed. "No, I am dying."

"No you're not. It's only a broken bone."

The girl pressed her lips together. "You're only a boy. You don't know anything. I am dying. I have been shot so many times . . ."

"Only once. And it went right through. Look, the border is just over the hill."

The girl was breathing hard. "Over this hill?"

"With hospitals and everything. If you can sit up I can help."

"Kid doctor," the girl snorted.

"My father was a doctor." Vithy reached for her good arm.

She looked thoughtfully at Vithy, glanced at her torn dress, the bandage and the palm leaves, and took his hand. He leaned back and pulled very hard. The girl gasped and shuddered, but she sat up.

"My shoulder . . ." She pushed the words between her teeth and clutched at her left elbow to support the arm.

"Can you stay up?" Vithy moved behind the girl with a strip from his shirt.

"I can't get up. Never."

"Yes." Vithy knelt and fed the strip through the shoulder hoops and pulled them towards each other, bracing the shoulders.

"That's better," the girl said in surprise.

"Good." Vithy tied a knot and made a wrist sling from his remaining strip.

The girl considered her arm. "Maybe it will do. What do we do now?"

"You have to get up and walk." Vithy stepped to the girl's side.

"Just a minute." The girl leaned away from her broken collar-bone and began to relax her face.

Vithy thought she almost looked beautiful, maybe the way Sorei would have looked in twelve years . . . "What's your name?"

"Saro. Didn't I tell you? Where are the others?"

"The people that were with you?"

86

"Yes. Ah, you weren't with us. You were hiding."

"They've gone."

"Gone?"

"I think they were sure you were dead."

"Well, I wasn't, was I?"

Vithy shrugged.

"I'll bite some heads off when I find them. All right." Saro clutched at Vithy's neck and pulled herself angrily to her feet. She swayed dangerously as all the colour drained from her face. "Ooh . . ." she said at last. "I'm so weak."

"You lost a lot of blood. Lean on me."

The small boy and the tall young woman moved slowly through the forest, her right hand pressing hard on his shoulder as he went ahead. In the beginning they talked a little, but they soon needed all their breath for walking. They struggled up the hill, and panted, and stopped and walked again. When something slithered across their path they did not change their pace at all. It was just too hard to slow down and then start again. But at last the hill began to flatten.

"Where's the border?" Saro gasped.

Vithy had to stop and put his hands on his knees before he had enough breath to answer. "Just a little bit."

"I can't see anything. You said the border would be here. Just here."

"It's close. It's easy to walk now. It's downhill."

"It's all right for you . . ."

But they walked down and level and even a little up through the lightening trees. Waking birds called in a ghost forest as shadows formed and began to shift. The path was no longer a winding tunnel through the darkness but a dusty crack across a rolling plain of trees and scrub.

But Saro was finished. She sagged slowly to the ground.

"Come on," he said. "We're almost there."

She shook her head. "We're lost. I'm staying here."

"You can't stay here." For an instant Vithy was looking at the remnants of the fine shirt the King had given him, the careful work with moss and palm leaf that Dad had taught him. He was thinking: she can't stay here and waste all that.

Then he saw Saro's face, exhausted and beaten, the way he must have looked to Mang in the paddy and in the forest so many times before. He sat down beside Saro. "We'll just rest here for a few minutes, ei?"

She sighed. "Where's the border? You're lost and we're just going round and round in circles. I'll stay here until someone finds me. Someone who knows where we are."

"You have to try . . ." Vithy's nose twitched. He stopped and frowned. "Sniff."

"What?"

Saro glared at Vithy, but she took a short breath through her nose.

Rice, tomatoes, meat, poultry, soya, tea . . .

"What is that?" said Saro.

"Breakfast," Vithy said.

12. 007

They stopped on the path when the woman by the pot saw them. She did not seem surprised, but she turned and shouted into the camp. Immediately men and women tumbled from shelters of branches, twigs and roughly woven grass and hurried towards them. For a moment Vithy was badly frightened, but there were no soldiers and most of the people seemed to be smiling. The woman who had shouted came to Saro's side and eased her down beside a tree, talking to her constantly and softly.

A man with a shock of white hair scrabbled his fingers in Vithy's hair. "Good, son, good. Are there any more coming?"

Vithy shook his head. "I don't think so."

The man nodded. "We heard the shooting. We hear it all the time. You were lucky."

"Lucky?" Vithy was looking at the pale girl as she sagged in the woman's hands.

"You reached us. Many don't. Yesterday five people were shot no more than four hundred metres from the camp. We brought a big boy in to the hospital but he was shot in the head. He won't live, but your girl will."

So it was that close. But was it over, even now? "Then this is Thailand?" Vithy asked. There were no signs, no fences to mark a border.

The man scratched his cheek. "Near enough. It's the closest most of us are going to get."

"This is not the border?" He was not going to be stopped now, was he?

Two men hurried to Saro with a much-used stretcher, unfolded it and gently eased Saro on top. She seemed to have fallen asleep.

"Oh yes, this is the border. The end of Cambodia. Now the Thais and the Red Cross feed us. You better follow your sister before you lose her."

Vithy started to tell the man that Saro was not his sister, but she was being carried rapidly into the camp and he didn't want to be left alone any more. He ran after the stretcher.

The two men walked swiftly into a growing city of shelters, relying on people moving out of their way as they approached. But they slowed suddenly as Vithy caught them, and began to skirt an open area with a few shelters and some sacks of rice.

"What is this place?" Vithy asked the rear stretcher bearer.

"The camp, or that?" The stretcher bearer nodded at the open area where about a dozen men in ragged shirts were squatting, working at something. "The camp is Nong Samet. The Thai army calls it 007. They think it is very funny like the super spy in the films. You see the films? Nong Samet is 007 because there is always trouble here. And *that* is most of the season."

The ragged men were cleaning their guns.

"Khmer Rouge?" Vithy whispered.

The stretcher bearer nodded. "It's all right now; they don't do anything during the day. They're here for food and maybe recruits to fight the Viets. Just keep clear of them."

Vithy shuffled so the stretcher was between him and the ragged men. He looked over his shoulder and wondered whether he would ever get away from them.

But the rest of the camp was made up of people, not soldiers. The shelters became thatched huts, occasionally with a roof of heavy blue plastic. Children weaved across the path with yokes of kerosene tins full of water. Women hung shirts and trousers on lines running from huts to trees and men talked gravely in circles around low fires. Nobody paid much attention to the stretcher.

They reached a dirt road, turned along it and stopped outside a large building with a wall of sticks and a roof like a circus tent of blue plastic. There were two four-wheel-drive vehicles parked under a tree outside the hospital. Two men bustled from the hospital, a Thai and an American, and took the stretcher from the tired bearers.

"Shot?" said the American, in English. He realised what he had said the moment he had said it and fumbled for the Cambodian words.

But Vithy nodded in understanding and groped for the English words. "Ei, she has . . . Is she well?"

The American looked at Vithy in surprise. "I think so kid. Just tag along."

Vithy followed the American and the stretcher into the blue light of the hospital. The American called to a nurse: "Tai Wan, give the kid a drink and show him a cake of soap."

91

The nurse, a tired Chinese girl of twenty, steered Vithy to a plastic barrel of cold water over a plastic sink. Five minutes later the sink was awash with evil-looking black water. The nurse found him a cheese sandwich and he was trying hard to eat it slowly when the voice of a woman boomed across the hospital, in English.

"Hey, who the hell's done this?"

"Must be the kid. He brung her in," said the American.

Alarmed, Vithy peered into the main ward. A woman in a blue smock, almost as huge as her voice, was glaring at him from behind thick glasses. Saro was on a bench beside the woman and people were lying on mats on the earth. Vithy ducked out of sight.

"Boy . . .!" The big woman's bellow was shaking the hospital.

Vithy turned to run, but the nurse was clutching for him. What had he done? What was wrong? He shouted wildly and kicked out at the nurse. The nurse screeched, but she had his arm now and she wouldn't let go. He hurled his body away from her and he was free and running . . .

The American plucked him from the air and carried him backwards towards the huge woman, his legs thrashing the air. He was dumped on a chair.

"Now," the huge woman raised her finger like a club, and pointed. "You just stay there. Right?"

Vithy stayed where he was put.

"He speaks English," the American said.

Vithy froze in the chair. At that moment a black

terror was sweeping over him. It was as if everything that had happened since his flight through the
forest with Mang was a dream, and now he was back
in the paddy again.

"Oh, you do that too? Speak English?" the huge
woman said.

Vithy looked rigidly ahead. He was going to use
the stock defence Mang had taught him in the
paddy. He was going to play dumb, but he knew it
was far too late.

"You *don't* speak English?"

Vithy did not move a muscle.

"It's a pity, because my Kampuchean is very bad
and I'd like to talk."

They even call Cambodia Kampuchea, thought
Vithy. Like the Khmer Rouge.

The huge woman sighed. "Oh, that." She waved
a bright little knife at Vithy, then beyond at the wall.
"Over there is Kampuchea, where you came from.
This is Thailand. We don't punish people for what
they know."

Vithy realised he was staring at a bottle of blood
suspended over Saro and followed a red tube
running from the bottle to her arm to focus on the
huge woman. Funny thing, close up the woman
seemed to shrink a little. She was still very big, but
she was not huge any more.

"I'm Dr Betty Harris," the woman said, now
keeping her eyes on Saro's body and her voice very
low. "You've got nothing to be frightened of here."

Dr Harris carefully lifted the palm leaves, then the
moss from Saro's shoulder, and studied the wound.
"I think Khao I Dang, eh, Frank?"

93

"Sure. And this time we can do something." The American held Saro up a fraction as Dr Harris swabbed the wound clean. Everything calm and efficient.

"You know you saved your sister's life," Dr Harris said.

Vithy frowned and again decided to leave the error alone. "She's all right, perhaps," he said, in English.

"She will be. Just a small scar. Sutures."

"I am very . . ." Too late Vithy realised what he was saying.

"Yes, I know. Glad."

And it didn't matter at all. For the first time Vithy began to feel that he had really crossed the border.

"What's your sister's name?"

"Sorei—Saro. Saro." Vithy flushed.

Dr Harris looked up at Vithy for a moment. "All right. And you?"

"Vithy."

"All right, Vithy. We're going to take Saro to a better hospital at Khao I Dang this afternoon and I think you'd better come along."

"Where's Khao I Dang? Is it on the border?"

"Almost on the border, but it's not as close to the border as this. Why?"

"I've got to find my brother."

"You were separated?"

"Yes."

"When?" Dr Harris' fingers were moving gently over Saro all the time.

Vithy hesitated. "Two weeks." Yes, it was only that long ago.

Dr Harris nodded. "That is not so bad. So many people come to the camps and look for wives and families they have not seen since the first war ended. Where did you last see your brother?"

"In a forest near Phnom Penh."

Dr Harris frowned at Saro. "You've been together all that distance?"

Vithy did not answer.

"Frank, you might as well take him over to the cafe. He might be lucky."

"Now?"

"I'll clean up."

Frank stripped off his gloves and found a spare green smock for Vithy to use as a shirt. He led Vithy from the hospital, getting some of his story while they strolled along the dirt road.

Vithy stopped to watch several men hurling themselves about in a wild game of volleyball beside several concrete tanks of water.

"You used to play?"

"Not much. I was too little. But Mang was very good."

"Ah. Do you see him?"

"No."

They skirted the Nong Samet morning market, five women with some vegetables and some shreds of meat, and passed two men repairing old bicycles under a tree. They stopped before the second biggest building in Nong Samet, a thatched hut of lashed stick walls, a low verandah and a painted sign that moved in the breeze, proudly announcing that this was the Café de la Bohème. A few men slouched against stripped poles and waited for Frank to speak.

95

"This is—ah—Muong Vithy," Frank fumbled in Cambodian. "He's looking for his brother."

A man in an open black waistcoat smiled at Vithy, showing the glint of gold in his teeth. "We'll see. You leave him here."

Frank nodded. "Thank you." He turned to Vithy. "You come back to the hospital early in the afternoon. Okay? Otherwise you'll miss your sister."

The man with the gold tooth beckoned Vithy into the café. Rectangular tables covered in tightly-pinned blue plastic sat against the glassless windows with hard wooden benches on either side. The floor was hard-packed and thoroughly-swept earth. There was only one decoration in the café but it sent a shiver down Vithy's spine.

Above the bench which separated the tables from the simple kitchen was a crude painting of Angkor Wat, the same grey stone colonnades and lotus-bud towers that marked a rich and happy time for Mum and Dad but now was nothing more than a desolate memory. He shifted his eyes from the painting and pretended it wasn't there.

"Now sit down, Vithy." The man with the gold tooth motioned to a bench. "Would you like some tea?" A woman with laugh wrinkles around her eyes pushed through the men, carrying a large pot and a few cracked cups. "She is Madame Bohème," the man said and laughed. "And I am Sokhar. Now, about your brother. You do not want to find anyone else, as well?"

"No." Vithy shook his head.

"I understand," the man said sadly. "What is your brother's name?"

97

"Mang. Muong Mang." Vithy searched Sokhar's face for recognition but found nothing but a frown.

Sokhar looked around at the others, shrugged and took a big black book from a younger man. He slammed it open, showing yellow pages with an endless list of names, many of them crossed out or with initials written over them.

"When do you think he arrived?"

"Maybe a week ago."

Sokhar riffled through the pages almost to the end, then ran his finger quickly down the list. "He might not be on the list. We try to keep up, but it is very hard. People come and go all the time. No, he is not there."

Vithy sagged on his elbows. Suddenly he was very tired.

"But I'll put you down." The man scribbled. "How do you know he came here?"

"He said he would come to the border."

"It's a long border."

"I know." Vithy's voice was weighted with lead.

"Where did you come from?"

"Near Phnom Penh."

"A long way."

Someone said: "He might be dead."

Sokhar said, "Shut up Khieu," very quickly but the damage was done.

"No he isn't!" shouted Vithy. "He's smart and he's fast and they'd never catch him . . ."

"Of course he's not dead." Sokhar patted Vithy on the shoulder. "There are many camps, and he may still be coming. You were very fast."

Vithy relaxed a little. With the truck and the bike

98

and the cart he had been lucky. Maybe little kids can be faster than big kids. So he wasn't going to find Mang just like that, but imagine his face when he finally reached the border to find his little brother waiting for him . . .

Sokhar stood up and studied Vithy. "When did you last sleep?"

Vithy looked at him blankly. He couldn't remember.

Sokhar led Vithy from the Café de la Bohème without a word. The boy was pushed into a nearby hut and onto a matting bed. Someone said something to him but he was too far away. He could feel the roughness of the matting on the side of his face but that was all . . .

Almost immediately Sokhar was shaking his shoulder. "It is three o'clock. You must leave."

Vithy blundered out of the hut and along the track while Sokhar told him, no, Mang wasn't in Nong Samet, 007. He'd checked while Vithy was asleep, but he would keep on looking.

Saro was lying in one of the vehicles, still asleep. A few nurses sat facing her. Dr Harris helped Vithy into the front, next to Frank.

"The army wants us out of here before the sun gets low," Dr Harris said in a troubled voice.

They drove across a huge moat which fenced 007 from the rest of Thailand, across a deserted paddy, past a shelled house and into the hills.

Vithy thought he heard shots behind him.

13. THE HOSPITAL

Vithy awoke slowly to a gentle sun on his face, the rich tang of rice and fish and the bright din of children chattering. He opened an eye.

"Hello." A gentle woman smiled at him and spoke in soft Cambodian with a French lilt. She squatted easily before him and offered a steaming bowl. "We thought you were going to be asleep until the rainy season." A small boy with a shaven head laughed from the eating mat.

Vithy sat up and winced. His legs and back did not want to move any more. And the sun was terribly high. "Excuse me," he said, "am I still at the border?"

"You are at Khao I Dang, in my house." The woman tempted him by swaying the bowl under his nose. "I'm Ponary."

He weakened and accepted the bowl hurriedly. "Thank you for breakfast."

"Yes, well it's really lunch . . ."

"Tomorrow's lunch!" giggled the bald little boy and the dozen children around him shrieked with laughter.

"You slept for a day and a half. You needed it," said Ponary.

Half a bowl, or two minutes later Vithy had cleared his mouth just enough to ask Ponary politely if all the noisy tribe around the mat were her family.

Ponary laughed. "And there are five other boys out building a house. All my family. Until an uncle or a mother crosses the border and finds them."

"Oh." Vithy filled his mouth with rice. He could think of nothing else to say.

"But *you* have family here, haven't you?"

Vithy stopped chewing and looked up. He half expected Mang to rise from that pile of children.

"Your sister, Saro."

Vithy dropped his eyes to the bowl. "How is she?"

"Good. You can go to the hospital and visit her this afternoon."

Over lunch Vithy got to know most of the children, particularly Sen, the boy with the shaven head. Sen had been in Ponary's house for no more than a month, but he was considered an 'old boy'. Sen was only a few months younger than Vithy, but Vithy could not shake off the idea that Sen was just a kid, a baby brother. Sen joined the other children as they laughed and joked but Vithy could only wear a weak smile like a mask. He was too old.

After the meal the younger children thundered out of the house to slide down a dusty slope on a bent sheet of corrugated iron, and Sen led a reluctant Vithy to the hospital.

Sen stopped in a broad quadrangle bordered by long buildings, each one twice the size of the hospital at 007, hemmed by small flower gardens and facing a wheezy loudspeaker on a pole. "That's it," Sen said, pointing ahead. "And that's my hospital too."

"Oh." Vithy recognised Dr Harris sitting in the sun drinking a cup of tea and he wanted to go somewhere else.

"See?" Sen bowed his head so Vithy could see the curved scar that crossed his head almost from ear to ear.

"What happened?" Vithy stepped back in surprise.

"Oh, I got shot," Sen said very casually. "On the head."

Vithy stared. "Near 007?"

"Near what? Oh, you mean that kid that got shot a coupla days ago. Nah, wasn't me, I'm fit. An Aussie doctor took him off somewhere to die yesterday. I was hit a month ago. Got better in that hospital. They are tremendous doctors here. If they can't cure you here nobody can."

"Vithy! Sen!" Dr Harris stood up and waved the cup as if it were a flag.

Sen ran across the quadrangle to her and she caught him in a bear hug. Vithy trailed slowly in his wake.

"Good news, Vithy," Dr Harris beamed at him. "Saro's awake and she's got visitors. Your father has found you!"

For a moment everything had become granite and motionless. A statue of Dr Harris was holding a statue of Sen and they looked as if they were about to laugh. And some tea was hanging in the air between the tilted cup and the ground.

Then he was past them, through the door and

running into the shadowy building with his mouth wide open and his eyes alight.

There was a great carpet of mat beds with men and women lying quietly, looking at the roof or the tall metal fans. Light was only seeping into the building through the doorway and under the heavy sunblinds. Vithy stumbled in the dim light before he could see Saro with a tall man hunched by her mat.

Saro recognised him and frowned. "Oh. That boy."

The tall man turned and half-smiled.

And Vithy stopped and felt something tearing at his throat.

Of course the man wasn't his father. He couldn't be. He was *her* father. He had just forgotten.

"The doctor says I should thank you. Thank you," said Saro. "But why does she keep on calling you my brother?"

Vithy swallowed. He mumbled, quickly, "Must be a mistake."

"Yes. Well, I'll see you later. I want to talk to my father now."

The tall man looked up almost apologetically, then turned to Saro.

Vithy shuffled sideways towards the door. He didn't seem to be able to see properly any more.

Dr Harris caught him and steered him into the open. She found him a chair and sat opposite him without a word. She pulled a packet of barley sugars out of a pocket and offered them to him. There was no sign of Sen. He blinked at the sweets and shook his head.

She popped one into her mouth. "I take these to

stop myself smoking." She closed the packet and put it away. "Saro. She's not your sister, is she?"

Vithy shrugged.

"You should have been left down at 007, Nong Samet, shouldn't you?"

Vithy stared at his knee.

"Shouldn't you?"

"Yes."

"That's a bit better. Look, we can use you here, but no more lies, all right?"

Vithy nodded.

"Why did you want to come here?"

"I wanted to find my brother."

"Oh, yes. Him. What about the rest of your family?"

Vithy shook his head.

"Do you want to tell me what happened?"

Silence.

"Vithy, when I first came here I had done a long stretch at casualty in a city hospital, and I thought I'd seen and heard everything. Okay, that was then. Now, three months later, I really *have* heard everything. Everything that happened to you and your family has happened to hundreds of people in this camp. Share your load."

Vithy did not move.

Dr Harris looked at the rigid boy before her for a while, then sighed. "All right, we'll just have to find that brother of yours."

The next morning Dr Harris brought Vithy a small pile of paper on which he was to write a brief notice. Vithy wrote:

Would anyone who knows where is
Muong Mang, son of Muong Phi of
Sambor please say hello to Muong
Vithy at Hospital Two at Khao I
Dang.

Thank you,
Muong Vithy.

Dr Harris looked at the notice then had Vithy
translate it into English from the Khmer in which it
was written.

She looked at the translation for a while, then
nodded. "It's all right. Now give me twenty
copies."

"Twenty copies?" Vithy stared at his small notice
and multiplied it in his mind.

"For the other camps."

Vithy eventually finished his notices and gave
them to Dr Harris, to be taken to all the other
border camps in Thailand. Now all he could do
was wait.

But for Vithy waiting was going to be busy.
While he was writing his notices, Dr Harris had
found a spare green smock and Ponary had stitched
it down to his size. He trailed Dr Harris and Frank
around the hospital, feeling foolish as Saro stared at
him from her mat, but noticing the few warm
smiles that floated from the patients over the
doctors and settled on him.

Next day he woke from a wild chase through a
grotesque forest to the smell of soya and fish. He
realised that for the first time in a long, long time
he wasn't worried about what he was going to eat

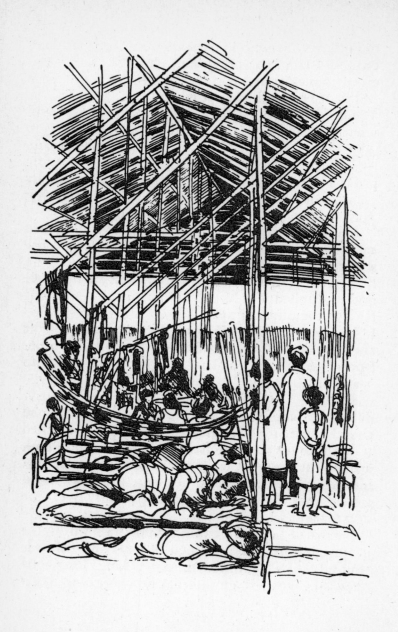

today. He opened his eyes to find Sen and three other boys staring at his green smock as if it was an emperor's cloak.

"You a doctor?" said Sen.

Vithy stretched, and yawned. "Oh, I lend a hand when they need me."

"Hoi!" said Sen, impressed.

But Ponary looked in. "Hoi, surgeon! You better get washed before the operation, eh?"

"Operation?" said Vithy.

"Breakfast."

But Vithy arrived at the hospital after breakfast eager, nervous and almost running past the loud-speaker as it tried to sing. For the first time since he had been marched from his home he was wanted, not just a number to feed and get work from, but because of the things he, Muong Vithy, could do. It wasn't until later that he began wondering if there was anything special he could really do in the hospital.

For a start Dr Harris was not at the hospital. Nor was Frank. In fact no one at the hospital that morning seemed to know why he was there or what he was supposed to do.

"Dr Harris?" said a nurse called Coldstream who sounded like a general. "She's at the border this morning. Might be in this afternoon. D'you want something?"

"Dr Harris says that I am to help."

"In the hospital?"

"Yes."

"Ah well . . . Can you wash up?"

Washing, drying, sweeping, adjusting the

shades, polishing pots. Nurse Coldstream could find all the work in the world for Vithy to do in the hospital and nothing that needed him especially to do it. The patients watched him in silence, judging his movement with the broom and his clumsiness with the screens. After several hours of hard labour he didn't worry about the watching patients, not even Saro with her cocked nose. He was just too tired to care.

Dr Harris didn't come to the hospital in the afternoon and there was no message from Mang during the day. Vithy trudged back to Ponary's house, ignored Sen with his rattan ball, ate and slept.

The following day Dr Harris was back in the hospital. She was peering into one of the pots Vithy had cleaned and polished with Nurse Coldstream by her side. She looked up and Vithy felt his stomach drop.

"Vithy, you clean these?" said Dr Harris.

"Um, yes . . ."

"Nurse Coldstream is glad I brought you from Nong Samet. Good job."

Vithy flickered a smile uncertainly across his face as he began to understand what Dr Harris was saying, then he grinned at Dr Harris, Nurse Coldstream and the entire hospital.

Dr Harris led Vithy into the ward and stopped before an old woman on a mat and pressed her hands together before her, bowing slightly, saying, "*Choumreap sour, lok,*" or, "Good day, madam."

The old woman nodded at Dr Harris without smiling and muttered, "*Choumreap sour.*"

Dr Harris turned to Vithy. "And this is where you come in. I'm afraid my knowledge of Khmer has just about run out. Please introduce us."

Vithy squatted by the old woman's mat and pressed his hands together in polite greeting. In Khmer he said, "Good day, madam. My name is Muong Vithy from Sambor. This is Doctor Harris and she wants to help you."

The old woman looked at Vithy with new interest, then her eyes glittered across to Dr Harris. "I am Tevoda, but there is nothing you can do for me."

Vithy turned to Dr Harris. In English he said: "This is Tevoda and she says there is nothing we can do for her."

Dr Harris frowned. "Of course we can do things for her. Ask her why she says this."

"What is wrong?"

"I am dying."

Vithy rocked back on his heels in silence.

"Well?" Dr Harris said.

Vithy translated.

"Rubbish. Tell her she is only a little sick in the belly and when we cure it she will be bounding about like a deer in no time at all."

Vithy translated and Tevoda actually smiled for a moment, but her face sobered. "How does she know these things? I am not carrying a baby."

"She is not a midwife. She is a doctor. She knows everything."

"How can that be? She is only a woman."

"They teach women everything now. In universities and colleges."

"Everything?"

"Everything."

"Where?"

"Everywhere. Even in Phnom Penh girls were at the university. My sister, Sorei, was going to go to the university at Phnom Penh when she got through high school . . ." Vithy petered out.

Tevoda nodded. "Ah. That is before the wars. Everything is before the wars . . ."

Dr Harris intruded. "Vithy, just what are you and Tevoda talking about. I feel left out."

"Oh, I am sorry," Vithy said. "Tevoda was asking me about you." Tevoda nodded and smiled at Dr Harris, with new respect in her eyes.

Dr Harris smiled back. "You must be doing it well. Go on."

"Where does this doctor come from?" Tevoda asked.

"I think—America?" Vithy looked up at Dr Harris.

Dr Harris caught the universal word 'America' and shook her head. "Australia is closer."

"Storyla?" Tevoda frowned then shrugged. "No matter," she said in English.

"Good. Let's get down to work."

After that the doctor's round went smoothly. With Vithy as a sympathetic mouthpiece, Dr Harris probed, tapped, listened to and dosed Tevoda, and Tevoda was willing to admit that she might not be dying at the moment. Then there was the boy, Vithy's age, who had just lost a leg and Dr Harris was trying to tell him he would walk again with an artificial leg, a girl with a fever, five thin

110

young men recovering from rickets, ten people from eight to forty with injuries and wounds they had suffered in the border camps. And there were more. At the end of the day Vithy was exhausted but he had begun many friendships.

Dr Harris stopped him in the yard outside the hospital. "It was a good day, Vithy. Thank you very much."

Vithy suddenly felt embarrassed. "Ah, it is a good job you give me, Dr Harris."

"Rubbish. Do you know how hard we have to look to find someone who knows English, Khmer and a little bit of medicine as well? You're a handy lad, Vithy."

Vithy glowed and scratched at a knuckle. "Thank you, Dr Harris."

"Oh I think we can drop that outside the hospital. Betty will do."

"Ah, well . . ."

"No, really."

Vithy shrugged and turned his toes into the dust. But he said, "Well, good afternoon Betty."

"Good afternoon Vithy. See you tomorrow."

Vithy skipped home to Ponary's house absolutely certain that the hospital would crash in chaos without him. It was a lovely feeling.

But there was still no sign of Mang.

14. THE BUS

Vithy did not explore Khao I Dang until the third week, and even then it took a remark from Sen to drive him from his comfortable little kingdom.

He had settled quickly into a contented routine and for a while he didn't want anything else. It was enough to sleep and eat at Ponary's house, work at Betty's hospital a two minute walk away, sometimes carry vegetables home from the crowded open market, and be surrounded by his people speaking his language. And not being afraid.

It hurt a little when Saro left the hospital without saying a word to him, but he'd seen Ko, the boy with one leg, race Betty fifty metres—and win. Tevoda had got up from her mat and bustled about the hospital to spread the latest gossip among the patients. Frank spent an afternoon teaching him how to play checkers, so he could teach patients. You could see new friends getting better every day.

And one day Betty came to him with an old transistor. "I don't suppose you would know how to make this work?" she said.

At Sambor, with Mang the Master hovering about and doing everything, he could not. At the Big Paddy, where you were taught not to think, he would not. But now he had fixed an outboard motor, built a bike and saved a girl's life. Now he could, would and did. Simply by scraping a dirty point under the battery plate.

"You're too much!" said Betty. "Where'd you learn all this?"

"Ah, we had a business under the house at Sambor," Vithy said. "We'd fix almost anything. Motorbikes, bicycles, radios, toys, anything."

"You and Mang?"

"Mainly Mang. I was the helper. It was a good business, but we had trouble all the time with Sorei's ducks."

"Ducks? My brother has a flock of them on his farm. Lovely eggs. But he only gets me on the farm as a sort of cheap amateur vet. What sort of trouble can those lovely birds give you?"

Vithy sighed. "All sorts. When they get through our fence they peck at our glue and oil and swallow our ball-bearings and when Dad chases them from his vegetable garden they all flap through our workshop. And then Dad is shouting and we're shouting and Sorei is running about screaming. So Mum sends us all from the house to cool off. When we get back we have a huge meal of duck and vegetables and rice."

Betty smiled. "That's the first time I've got you talking about your family outside Mang. They sound great."

A shadow passed across Vithy's face but Betty knocked it away with a quick peal of laughter. "Do you know I was once a duck? Really. The theatre group I was in decided to put on a pantomime with pirates, giants, singing cats and a dancing duck. Me. Everyone thought they had never seen such a

113

splendid-looking duck as me. I still feel I should have killed the director."

So Vithy had to tell of his Dad on the riverboat to Phnom Penh, dancing and playing his *khene*.

Vithy and Betty spent hours every day talking, in and out of the hospital. When she wasn't a doctor, Betty was becoming more fun to be with than Sen and for some strange reason she seemed to like Vithy almost as much as he liked her. The small area around the hospital was a great place to be and Vithy did not want to see any more of the sprawling camp.

But then Sen caught him watching some children kicking a ball around in the dust.

"Want a game?" asked Sen.

Vithy shook his head. Kids' games.

Sen sat beside Vithy. "Still nothing from your brother?"

"No. Are you waiting for anyone?"

Sen shrugged. "No. There's no one left to wait for."

"Oh."

"It's all right. This way I got nobody to worry about. There's just me and the camp and Ponary. That's all."

Vithy hunched over his knees and looked bleakly into the distance.

"Perhaps he's sent you a note."

"I am waiting for it."

"No, I mean he might have missed your note. He might have got here first and sent you a note on the bulletin board."

"Why would he do that? I told him where I am."

"He may not be looking at the bulletin board. He may have sent a message and now he's just waiting for you to read it. Have you seen the camp bulletin board . . ."

Vithy walked very fast from Sen, angry at his own stupidity. It seemed that the moment he didn't have to think to survive, he just didn't. When a silly kid comes up and tells you what you should have worked out weeks ago you ought to be kicked in the head.

He hurried down the dusty lanes between the huts, past the new skeletons of bamboo that Ponary's older children were helping turn into houses with windows and floors. He passed under the tall blue water tower, like some ancient dragon rearing above the camp, and past the few fibro-cement buildings. Everywhere loudspeakers were crackling and whooping at him. By the time he reached the front gate of the camp Vithy was realising that Khao I Dang was becoming a small city.

Vithy wandered into another hospital compound, Hospital One, and saw several buses parked beyond the gate before he was directed to a tall bamboo building. He had no trouble in finding the notice board. In a wide room filled with Khmer handicrafts, paintings, carvings, woven fabrics, a cluster of people swayed before a paper snowstorm tacked to a wall.

It took Vithy ten minutes to get close enough to the board to read the notices, and then he could not find his own notice, let alone a message from Mang. He stood before the board, continually jostled and trodden on, as he stared at sad little

116

notes on torn pieces of paper, coloured discs, photographs that were little more than grey blobs, and sometimes neat typed appeals. Calls from mothers to sons, sons to sisters, sisters to grandmothers, grandmothers to anyone in the family at all. And nothing for or from Vithy.

Until he saw 'Thank you, Muong Vithy' under a crinkled message. He removed the message, found another place for it and reread his own notice. Then he realised that all his own notices were on noticeboards like this and they were all probably covered like this one. They would probably never be read.

Vithy slouched to the door and stared at the long chain of parked buses without seeing them. Two loudspeakers shouted at each other. Mang must have reached the border now, but there was nothing he could do to reach him . . .

Vithy slowly began to see the people near the buses.

Beside the buses there was a far longer queue of quiet people with bundles at their feet or on their shoulders. They all looked tense and unhappy, almost frightened. A few soldiers, carrying guns on their shoulders, talked in small groups. It was as if the people were being forced to take this bus ride.

One soldier noticed that Vithy was staring at him and raised his arm to wave.

Vithy screamed and began to run.

15. Night of the Soldiers

Betty saw Vithy running a long way off. With his head down and his feet dancing desperately to stay under his careering body, he didn't know where he was going. Betty jumped from the Toyota and crouched, spread her hands, and caught him like a flung medicine ball.

He squirmed in her arms, shouted and kicked at her.

"Hey, hey." She pulled him to her, pressing him to her body, lifting him from the ground. "It's me, it's me . . ."

Vithy stopped kicking, but he would not open his eyes. "The bus," he kept saying. "The bus, the bus . . ."

"The buses at the front gate?" Betty was puzzled. "They don't do any harm."

Vithy jerked his head from side to side.

Betty put Vithy on the ground and bent forward so her head was very close to his. "Is it the people? They are just going to a transit camp nearer Bangkok. They want to go. They are just nervous. They are going to countries all over the world. To France, America, Britain, Australia . . . What's wrong?"

But Vithy just kept shaking his head.

Betty straightened and looked in the direction of

118

the front gate as if something strange and terrible was about to thunder down the road. She bobbed her head at Frank, who slowly drove away. Then she turned back to Vithy.

"Bus, Vithy? Just one bus that frightens you? Not a lot of buses?"

Vithy lifted his eyes to Betty. He looked at her for a long time, then nodded.

"I think we'd better talk now," Betty said.

The war in Cambodia hadn't really troubled the people at Sambor. One week there were Government soldiers, the next week there were Khmer Rouge and the fighting was somewhere downriver. But then the war came to an end.

"One night the soldiers came," said Vithy simply.

"And took your father," murmured Betty.

"Yes."

"In a bus filled with teachers, doctors, engineers and monks."

Vithy stared at Betty.

"We have heard it before. Many times. You are not alone."

Vithy looked away. That night was his, and his alone. That night even Mang was somewhere else.

A motor cycle had roared out of the shadows, throwing strange shapes across the kitchen as its headlight swayed in the window and grew. And stopped.

Dad had turned off the radio and was on his feet before the kicking at the door had started. He spoke to a soldier in a peaked cap outside the door, softly

119

so the soldier had to stop shouting and nobody in the house could hear what he was saying. Then he turned back to the family and smiled, but his face was like a dead fish. He said, "They want me to help them with a little job. For a while. Be good. Be careful . . ."

He touched Mum lightly on the cheek with his finger and walked away, towards a bus parked in the street, filled with silent watching faces.

And then he was gone.

Betty sighed and pressed her fingers over her eyelids. "That's not the end, is it?"

"They took Mang away."

"I thought you saw Mang only a few weeks ago."

"Yes. He came back."

"Yes?"

"Mang returned and tried to find Dad. He couldn't find him and the soldiers came again. They took our house and everything and marched maybe a hundred of us out of Sambor. We walked for a week. Sorei rode on Mang's back for most of the time. Then we stopped by an old ferry and some of us went across the Mekong and the rest just stayed where they were. Sorei, Mum and me, we went on the ferry but they kept Mang on the river bank. We could see him most of the way across the Mekong.

"We walked for few more days and stopped where a lot of people were chopping down trees to make a very big paddy. Mum and Sorei were taken to some huts and the men and the kids built huts for ourselves in another place. We didn't get much food. We got so tired one kid fell off the roof of one of the huts because he fell asleep on the thatch. We would have laughed but we weren't allowed to.

"I saw Mum a few times when we were all working in the big paddy. Sorei was working with Mum and she looked all right. A bit tired and dirty and sad, but she was all right. But Mum looked terrible. I got near Sorei and she said Mum had been sharing rice with her. Then Sorei was out on her own and I never saw Mum again. They took Sorei away two weeks later. Someone said a soldier asked her if she had learned to read and she said yes and she could do sums too . . ."

Betty was crumbling a clod of earth in her hands. "You—" She coughed to clear her throat. "You didn't see Sorei again?"

"'Course not. She was dead. Stupid girl." Vithy was now completely calm, as if he was talking about a boring movie he had seen last week, except that his shoulders and arms were shivering slightly.

"Okay." Betty steamrolled her words, keeping them flat and expressionless to match Vithy. "Just one more thing. How did Mang find you and lose you again?"

Some of the strain left Vithy's face. It was better now. "One day he just walked into the paddy with a few people and two soldiers. He just nodded at me in the beginning and he didn't speak to me at all for three days. Later he said he was just being careful, that's all. He said that was what you have to be all the time, careful and dumb. When I told him about Mum and Sorei he kept saying we had to go somewhere.

121

"Then the new war started in the mountains and trucks kept coming to our Big Paddy for rice. But there hadn't been enough rain for the Big Paddy and there wasn't enough rice for the trucks and us. The war came closer and sometimes we could hear the shells and soldiers started to take people into the forest and come back by themselves.

"One day the soldiers took us into the forest. But the soldiers were afraid of some shelling near us and we stopped in a small clearing. Suddenly Mang shouted to all the people, 'Run!', and we ran. We stayed together for a long distance with the soldiers chasing us but I got a sore foot and Mang led them away from me. He said he would come here."

Betty squeezed Vithy's shoulder for a moment, then let her hand drop. "So you came here. Right across Kampuchea, through jungles, bandits and a war, on the chance that you can find him."

"He is all I have."

16. THE KILLER

A few days later Vithy was shouting at Sen over the din of a loudspeaker on a pole when he stopped, listened and thought. He searched for Betty and found her watching some kids playing on the gravel slide. She looked deeply unhappy.

"Something is wrong?" he said, a little nervously.

Betty put a smile on her face, but it looked wrong. "Oh, just thinking about your family and you, Vithy. And, I guess, me."

"You said it does no good to think about that now."

"No, I wasn't thinking of the days of the soldiers and the Big Paddy. I said that now you've brought that out and looked at it you should throw it away. There is nothing else you can do with it. You don't forget but you don't have to remember all the time either. Okay, I said that, but you don't throw away good times too."

Vithy kicked at a pebble.

"I was thinking about your house at Sambor, with Mang and you revving old motorbikes, your mum and Sorei polishing the pots and your father chasing the ducks. It must have been wonderful."

Don't think about Big Paddy but remember Sambor. Vithy stood before Betty with a frown

123

and looked far beyond her. "It was noisy," he admitted.

"I'll bet. And there's you telling tales to little Sorei under the fig tree . . ."

And Vithy smiled. "She knew most of the stories. Sometimes she read her stories to me."

"It sounds very, very good. I'll tell you something, Vithy. I've got a little house in the suburbs. It's got a vegetable garden which hasn't been touched for six months, no pets and definitely no ducks. The neighbours would scream blue murder. I just rattle round the house like a pea in a thimble. I envy you your house in Sambor."

"You have no family?"

"You mean husband and kids? No, too much trouble. But I am not looking forward to going back to that empty house."

Vithy caught his breath. "Are you leaving?"

Betty leaned forward and rumbled Vithy's hair. "Not for a while, kid. I guess we've both got the same trouble. Just call us Lonely." She gave his head a playful cuff. "Anyway, what did you want?"

Vithy stood in the dust for half a minute until he was able to remember why he had wanted Betty this afternoon. "Oh, yes. Loudspeakers. Are they in *all* the border camps?"

"Well, most of them. Why? Oh, Mang."

"Can I send a message?"

"Why not?"

Vithy heard his message over the loudspeakers the following day. Everyone in the hospital and Ponary's house heard it and talked about it for

124

hours afterwards. Vithy knew his name and Mang's name were being broadcast all over the border all that week and he just had to listen for the answer.

It never came.

For weeks Vithy's message was sent regularly through the loudspeakers in the camps, but it was like listening down a deep well to the echoes of your voice. Vithy's world was only Ponary's house and the friendly little hospital and he was beginning to believe that was all it had ever been or would be.

But one day the hospital changed.

The youth was carried into the hospital late in the afternoon. He was unconscious, but two patients near his mat shuffled away and refused to be moved back. He had been shot in the shoulder.

Vithy stood at the foot of the youth's mat, looking at a face with black fat lips, heavy bones and wide-set eyes framed by a shock of tangled hair, and realised with a slight shock that the youth was not that much older than he was.

"Lovely, isn't he?" Betty pressed Vithy on the shoulder. "He comes from Nong Samet."

"What's his name?"

"No one knows. He wouldn't speak to us at all at the camp."

"Is he a soldier?"

Betty nodded. "I think he might be a bad one. He was shot by his friends."

That did not make sense. "Friends?"

Betty put her hand on Vithy's shoulder. "I'm sorry, Vithy, but we have to look after him. He's Khmer Rouge."

Vithy couldn't eat that night. When he slept he was being chased through the forest by a soldier with a peaked cap on a motor cycle. Ahead of him Dad and Mang were watching him from a parked bus, but he could not touch them. The bus was drifting sideways, always just beyond his reach . . .

When he woke up Vithy did not want to go back to the hospital. He wanted to stay with Sen and build houses or just play ball. He felt a little sick in his stomach, and he knew that if he went to the hospital today it would be one of the worst days of his life.

But he went because Betty was expecting him, and that was that.

The Khmer Rouge soldier was awake when Vithy entered the hospital, and he stared about him with carefully constructed contempt. Nurse Coldstream tried to help him with his morning rice but he shoved her back, grabbed the bowl and ate from it as if it were a mug.

"You don't do that to me, boy!" Nurse Coldstream shouted at the youth, but he looked up at her with ice in his eyes. Nurse Coldstream backed away, found something to do a long way away and stayed away.

"Come on, Vithy," Betty said. "Before we have real trouble."

Vithy followed the doctor to the youth's mat and squatted a little further away from him than with any other patient. The youth looked at Vithy with half-closed eyes and Vithy remembered the shooting the night before he had reached the border, the desperate rush of people through the undergrowth

126

and the screaming. Was this soldier there that night? He looked as though he would kill people as easily as snapping a twig.

"Ask him what his name is," Betty said.

Vithy moistened his lips. "I am Vithy. This is Dr Harris. What is your name?"

The youth's eyes flitted to Dr Harris and back again. He said nothing.

"We are trying to help you. What is your name?" Vithy rubbed his hands as he spoke. They had become moist.

The youth watched Vithy as if he was about to fall asleep. He began to smile at some private joke.

Betty clicked her tongue. "Tell the boy he's got a bullet through his shoulder and if we don't help him his arm will drop off."

Vithy translated. The youth's face did not change, but he was looking at Betty now and the smile seemed to be frozen.

"What's the name?"

The youth opened his mouth, but closed it again with enough force for Vithy to hear the teeth click.

Betty sighed. "I'm not going to play soldiers with you, boy. I want to change your bandage and have a look at that wound. If you co-operate, fine. If you don't, you get dropped at the border today. Now, do I get a look at that arm? Just nod your stupid head."

Vithy took some of the anger out of Betty's words in the translation. But the youth stared at him with a cold anger, blaming him, not Betty, for the words he was saying.

Vithy imagined a peaked cap on the youth's hard

128

face, and it fitted. He wanted to get up from the mat and run into the warm sun outside.

"Well?" said Betty. Vithy did not translate.

The youth very slowly nodded his head.

Betty motioned the youth to rise and helped him to his feet. She led him to a bench in an open space, sat him down and approached him with a pair of scissors. He widened his eyes before the long, gleaming blades, and tensed with a shudder as she began to snip carefully at his bandage.

"Now this will hurt a little . . ." Betty said softly. But Vithy forgot he was Betty's mouth. Her words were not translated.

Betty put the scissors behind her and gently tugged at the discoloured dressing under the youth's bandage.

The youth opened his eyes and shouted in anger.

Vithy remembered what he had been supposed to do and took a quick step forward.

Betty stopped tugging at the dressing but she was still looking at the wound, not at the face of the youth. "It's all right . . ." she said.

But it was all too late. With the stinging pain in his shoulder and the big woman still pulling at the bandage, the youth began to fight to escape. He twisted away from Betty, chopped at her hand and grasped her wrist.

"Hey!" she gasped.

He twisted her arm behind her back. She cried out in pain as he forced her to bend forward.

Vithy opened his mouth and he was back in the forest, running with Mang. And falling, with soldiers thrashing through the undergrowth around him.

Betty had sunk to one knee, with her hand pushed so far up her back she could touch her neck. She was trying to say something but she could do nothing but gasp and wheeze. She looked at Vithy and he felt utterly helpless.

The youth leant sideways and picked up the scissors, closing the long blades and gripping them like a knife.

The youth was suddenly wearing the peaked cap and was pushing Dad towards the bus . . .

Someone was shouting, shouting the length of the hospital, so loudly the building echoed. Betty and the youth and the bench swayed toward Vithy, gliding under him and the youth was looking up at him in alarm.

Vithy had the scissors in his hand and he twisted them from the youth's grip. The youth bucked desperately under Vithy, releasing Betty and reaching for his face. They rolled about the hospital floor, colliding with recoiling patients, the bench, a tray of medicines and a hard wooden pillar.

The noise in the hospital became a spreading storm. For an instant Vithy was on top of the youth and in control, then the youth punched him in the face with his good arm. Vithy reeled back, the youth had him down on the floor and by the throat. Vithy tossed, turned and punched wildly up at the youth. The youth let go and sagged back with his hand on his shoulder. Vithy pushed him down for the last time, straddled him, pinning both arms to the ground. He was surprised to see that he still held the scissors.

For a moment Muong Vithy balanced the scissors in his hand, and that youth had become all the soldiers who had destroyed his life and his family. The youth was the officer with the bus, the man who asked Sorei if she could read, the men who had shot at Mang in the forest. And he held a weapon in his hand . . .

But the youth was looking up at him.

He wasn't a soldier any more. He was just a hurt boy, so frightened there were tears in his eyes.

Vithy slowly lowered the scissors and felt a gentle hand on his shoulder.

"It's okay now," Betty said. "It's all over."

17. THE LUCKIEST BOY

Vithy walked out into the morning sun and sat down on a bench. He felt very cold and he couldn't stop shivering for more than half an hour. When Betty joined him she was wearing a sling.

"Thanks," Betty said.

Vithy tried to smile but failed. "You are hurt?"

"Nothing broken. I just have to give it some rest for a few days." She sat down beside him and for the first time seemed to be searching for words. "I have been meaning to speak to you . . ."

"Oh, yeah." That was before the fight. So long ago. Vithy kept on thinking how that fight might have ended. It frightened him very much.

"Have you heard anything of your brother?"

Vithy shook his head slowly. The speaker over his head spluttered. It seemed to be laughing at him.

"How long have you been looking for him now?"

"For a long time, I guess. Four months, maybe."

Vithy looked up as his voice wheezed tiredly over the loudspeaker. He had heard himself perhaps twenty times and he moved his lips to mime the old tape recording.

"Muong Mang. Muong Mang of Sambor, can you hear me? This is Muong Vithy, your brother. I am at Hospital Two in Khao I Dang, waiting for you . . . Please, if anyone has heard of Muong Mang of Sambor, please tell me, I am Muong Vithy at Hospital Two . . ."

"Four months?" Betty interrupted the loud-speaker. "That's a long time."

"Yes."

"What do you think?"

"I don't know." But he *did* know. He just wasn't admitting it.

"Well." Betty scratched her knee. "How long will you wait for him?"

Vithy shrugged.

"I finish here in three weeks." Betty spoke fast and looked away, as if talking to the loudspeaker.

Vithy stared at Betty. "But you said that wasn't going to be for a long while."

"That was a long while ago, Vithy. Other doctors want to come here to help. I must make room for them."

Vithy hunched his shoulders and gently shook his head. He had lost Betty as surely as if the Khmer Rouge soldier had succeeded with those scissors. And this time there was nothing he could do. He was alone again.

"Sorry, Vithy," Betty said.

But no more than two hours later Betty stormed into Ponary's house, grabbed Vithy by the shoulders, sat him on a bed and said: "What the hell, kid. Want to come home with me?"

Vithy could not understand the woman. "What?" he asked stupidly.

133

"Home. Australia. Sydney. House full of weeds."

"Oh."

"If you can't find Mang of course."

"Go to Australia? It's a terrible long way."

"There are a lot of Kampucheans—Cambodians —in Sydney. Do you want to come? If I can get you out?"

"How will Mang find me?"

Betty didn't say anything for a while. "Tell you what we'll do. Just forget about Mang. Just for a moment. Now, without Mang, would you rather stay here in Khao I Dang or come with me?"

Vithy was being asked to think the unthinkable. Making any big plan without Mang was as silly as paddling a boat with a spoon. Planning to live, not across the border but half a world away, was paddling a boat with a spoon in a flood. But apart from Mang there was only Betty.

"Australia," Vithy said, and felt cold.

After a few days Betty came to the hospital and took down all Vithy's family history, his education, medical details and muttered odd things about the Embassy. She went to the Embassy in Bangkok with all the forms filled in as Vithy made a new tape for the loudspeaker. He heard it transmitted over the speakers after a news bulletin about Nong Samet being the centre of a border battle.

In the evening of the next day Betty and Frank caught Vithy outside Ponary's house within minutes of each other, as if they had been racing each other. Betty arrived first in a squeal of rubber and a cloud of dust.

134

"You, Muong Vithy, are the luckiest boy in the world today!" Betty leapt from the commandeered Toyota.

It had been a long hard day and Vithy didn't feel any luckier than yesterday or any other day. "What?"

Betty squatted unsteadily before him. "I've just come back from the Embassy, and they're not really that bad when you get them to move. So I found out some pretty wonderful things . . ."

And Frank's old Land Rover rolled to a stop behind Betty's Toyota. He got out and waved at Betty and Vithy, but Betty did not even see him.

"Now you can go to Australia—just like that!" Betty snapped her fingers. "Well, almost."

"Hi, kids," Frank said.

"And you didn't need me to sponsor you . . ."

"So ignore me, already," Frank said. "I've only found Mang."

18. MANG?

Betty and Vithy stared at Frank for a moment. Then Vithy began to smile.

Betty frowned. "Are you sure, Frank?"

"I met him."

The smile became a grin.

"Where?" Betty seemed puzzled.

"Nong Samet. 007. He heard Vithy's message yesterday. Skinny Khmer, but big. Said he was Muong Mang from Sambor."

And the grin became a whoop. Vithy leapt to his feet and hugged them both. But then the grin faded from Frank's face. "I guess he won't be going to Australia after all. Sorry, Betty."

Betty waved him down. "It's what's right for the boy that counts. We'll go and see this Mang tomorrow."

From a distance 007 did not seem to have changed at all since Vithy had last seen it, months ago. But the Café de la Bohème had been scorched and a few Khmers were patiently filling in a great hole, a crater, between the café and the hospital. On a distant rise the drab brown of the huts had been cut into by a wedge of black where a fire had raced from one hut to many of its neighbours.

Vithy jumped from the Toyota and scanned the

people around the hospital. But there was no sign of Mang. "What happened?" he asked, trying to control his anxiety.

"Another fight." Betty stepped out behind him. "Nasty one."

Vithy nodded. He could feel sympathy for these hundreds of people who could not escape from war, but he was here to finally find Mang, and that was the best thing in the world. To see him and touch him after all those months of doubt and wandering and waiting . . . He thought he might never let Mang out of his sight again.

"Well, hello fellah." Frank was greeting someone on the other side of the vehicle.

Vithy turned to look but the cabin blocked his view.

"Hi, Mang," Frank said warmly.

Vithy started to run around the Toyota.

"You come to take me away, yes?"

Vithy stopped.

A tall Khmer in rags, young, thin, with a nervous voice and a light smile playing across his face.

Not Mang.

"Not yet," Frank was saying, his voice echoing in Vithy's head. "But here's someone to see you . . ."

"You don' understand. I got to go with you." The young man glanced at Vithy as he waved his hands at Frank. "I am Muong Mang from Sambor, I got to see Veethy in Khao I Dang . . ." Then he looked back at Vithy. Vithy and the man stared at each other in silence until Vithy shook his head and ran blindly through the camp.

Betty found Vithy two hours later, sitting on a hill outside the camp, facing Kampuchea.

"I am sorry," she said. "It was a rotten trick. He got frightened in the fighting here so he thought he would get into safe Khao I Dang by pretending to be somebody else. Never mind that we'd know in the first hour in Khao I Dang. I wanted to kick him right round the camp."

"Doesn't matter," Vithy said.

"You're not angry at all, are you?" Betty was puzzled.

"What's the good?"

She winced. "Do you want to go back?"

He shook his head. He had been looking at the distant blue trees of Cambodia, remembering Dad flying a fierce kite with Sorei giggling on his shoulder, Mum laughing and dancing the old legends with a lamp balanced on her head. And Mang, always remember Mang on a dragon of a boat, striding down the river in a cloud of flying spray with the other boats snapping at his tail. But the memory was all that remained.

"I don't know if I'm doing the right thing," Betty was saying, apparently to herself. "But after that boy pretending he was Mang . . ."

Vithy stood up and brushed his shorts. "Mang's dead," he said.

19. HOME

For two days Vithy was left alone. Betty disappeared from Khao I Dang. Frank went to other
border camps and Ponary, even Nurse Coldstream,
watched him with worry in their eyes. He didn't
mind. He had brought his dying hope of ever
finding Mang into the open, and he had killed it.
Now he didn't want to share his final grief with
anyone.

He could sit down in Khao I Dang and taste the
earth that had rimmed his lips when he heard that
single shot in the forest. And he could still hear the
echo through the trees and the silence. That was
real. The rest, the King's encouragement, the tale
of whistling in Siem Reap, even the discovery of
Mang's railway lines . . . they were no more than
the wild dreams of a silly little boy. There was
nothing left.

Then Betty came back, and Vithy was jerked
from his sorrow by an accelerating rush to leave
Khao I Dang and Thailand. He was filling in and
signing white forms, pink forms, yellow forms,
green forms, without understanding what any of
them meant. Betty took a sample of his blood,
shone a torch into his eyes, pounded his chest and
stabbed him with needles. Australia wasn't worth
this.

But one day Betty said: "You're off the day after tomorrow. Get ready."

Vithy said goodbye to Sen and Ponary and Ko—who was racing doctors and journalists and winning—and many others. He shook hands with Frank for the last time as Betty ushered him towards the waiting buses.

"Sorry about that Mang stunt, son," Frank said. "It stank."

"Not your fault." Vithy shrugged and tried to smile.

"Am I doing the right thing, Frank?" Betty asked suddenly.

Frank smiled awkwardly. "You'll know soon enough. Good luck, Vithy."

Vithy turned, swallowed his old terror and joined the queue for the buses.

The bus took him to another camp and for three days he thought Betty had changed her mind about him. Then Betty arrived with documents, more papers to sign and he was told he was free. He left the last camp with Betty in the late afternoon and went to Bangkok.

In the one day he saw Bangkok he was astounded by the size of the city and a little frightened by the din. The temples were like Phnom Penh, but bigger. The river was about the same, but dirtier with huge freighters anchored in the middle. In the streets more cars, buses, trucks and motor bikes than in all old Cambodia coughed and blared at each other, with small boys trying to clean windscreens. And there were great buildings blocking out the sky. Vithy had seen pictures of New York

140

and other cities but he hadn't really believed a city could be this big. That evening Vithy and Betty took off for Australia.

As the 'plane roared down the streaked concrete and slid into the air Betty squeezed Vithy's hand. "Still thinking of Mang?"

Vithy was trembling as houses became roofs, then tiny boxes. He didn't hear her.

"You know, this is not the end. He might still be alive . . ."

Vithy turned to her and stared into her eyes. "No," he said slowly and deliberately. "No more."

Betty sat back in her seat in silence. She looked hunted.

Vithy's first five minutes of flight frightened him, but he kept quiet and in the next two hours his fear became fascination. He watched the city become paddy, bright water, jungle then a great plain of nothing else but water. He remembered an old man in Sambor who talked of spirits, *phis*, in the trees and the hills, and talked about the edge of the world. He didn't believe it then, and he tried not to believe it now, but he could not stop himself from nervously looking for a mighty waterfall. But the sun set and the plane began to circle the glittering lights of Singapore. He fell asleep.

When he woke the 'plane was flying again, but there were no jungles, no seas, no cities. There was nothing but a great red desert, stretching from horizon to horizon with low ranges rippling like a child's finger painting.

"Where are we?" he asked, dreading the answer.

"Australia. Isn't it beautiful?"

141

"Yes," Vithy said. He thought, no trees, nothing. How can I live here?

But after a short while grey clouds slid under the plane, leaving it alone in the sky.

"What is going to happen to me, Betty?" Vithy asked.

"I haven't told you enough, have I? For a start you'll be going back to school—and you'll be meeting people."

"School?" Suddenly Australia was not all that strange and terrible. He knew and could understand what school was all about, from before the wars. "Am I going to stay with you?"

For a moment Betty seemed to hesitate, but she smiled. "Don't you worry. It's all fixed up."

That wasn't enough. "Are you going to be my mother?"

Betty turned to Vithy in surprise and saw the lonely fear in his eyes. She took his hand. "Vithy, I am anything you want me to be for as long as you want."

Red lights flicked on on the 'plane asking passengers to extinguish cigarettes and fasten their seat belts. The captain began to talk about Sydney and the plane dipped into the grey clouds.

A dirty fog for half a minute, with drops of water racing across the windows. Then the city. Lakes, estuaries, rivers of flat bronze water, buildings fenced by lush trees and bordered by water. Buildings from the mountains' edge to the white curl of the ocean. Buildings rising in a great hump from the ground, still rising in shining parapets and a golden tower reaching for a hazy sun.

"It can't be that big," Vithy said quietly.

The 'plane descended until the wheels squealed shortly and Vithy was in Australia.

Vithy remembered Cambodia and his family as he passed through customs. He had lost his country and, far worse, his family. That was a sadness that would never leave him, but perhaps he could be happy here.

"I am going to be a doctor," Vithy told Betty as they passed through customs.

"Ah-huh," Betty said, looking around her. She seemed to be biting her lip.

"I will work hard, Betty. Thank you for bringing me."

Betty smiled. "I didn't bring you, really. I just helped. You would have got here on your own, given a little time. I tried to tell you."

Vithy shook his head.

"Oh yes. The Immigration people bend over backwards to help people with relatives here . . ."

Betty raised her head to meet the eyes of a youth standing clear of the customs barrier. She hesitated and watched Vithy.

Vithy stopped.

The youth before him was a stranger. He was gaunt, with lines on his face and a pale wash under the brown of his skin. He stood with a slight hunch, as if he had not yet the strength to stand up straight. An ugly scar above his ear marked the wound made by a bullet very near Nong Samet, 007, four months ago. He had been a nameless and unconscious body, very close to death, when he was taken from Nong Samet to Khao I Dang. He

143

was no more than a number when a specialist on extended leave decided that it was just possible to save his life and took him carefully to Bangkok. He was a number scrawled on a yellow card when he was flown to a team of neuro-surgeons in Sydney for a ten hour operation. He stopped being a number when he woke after sleeping for three months and told a tired doctor his name. He was still very weak.

A stranger. But somehow not quite . . .

The young man began to cock his face for an old lop-sided grin, but Vithy suddenly saw through the lines and the weariness. He would recognise this stranger in a monkey mask. He gave a whoop and a yell and flapped his arms in the air, and leapt at the man.

The stranger crouched, and caught Vithy, and pressed him to his shoulder.

He said: "Hello, little brother."